D1524140

BELONG TO YOU

BELONG TO YOU

Cheyenne McCray

Pink zebra publishing
Scottsdale, Arizona

CHAPTER 1

Anna Batista sat next to Chandra Johnson in the audience in the high school auditorium as they watched the debate between the two candidates for the office of Yavapai County Sheriff.

The incumbent, Sheriff Mike McBride, was facing off with his opponent, Chad Johnson. The debate between Sheriff McBride and Chad had been a heated one so far. Anna knew very little about the history between Mike and Chad, but she knew from Chandra that some bad blood between them went back a long way.

"Sheriff McBride, what is your opinion on the escalation of drugs and violence in Prescott and the county as a whole?" the moderator asked.

While Mike responded to the question, Anna cocked her head to the side and appraised him. She admired his strength and comfort under fire. He didn't act or talk like a politician and his down-to-earth demeanor and relaxed personality had made him popular, along with his sense of humor. One of the reasons she was certain he had been elected to county sheriff in the first place was his likability. He was tough but friendly, firm yet fair.

The fact that Mike was a dead-sexy cowboy was only the icing on the cake. All six-one of him was muscular, and his skin was deeply tanned from being out in the sun so often. His features were carved, his eyes a warm brown. Damn, but he was hot. The fact that he was in uniform didn't hurt at all.

Nice, she thought. *Very nice.*

A frown creased her face as she watched Chad Johnson take his turn at answering the same question about the escalation of drugs and violence in the area. Chad wore a business suit and bold red tie. He couldn't look more different than Mike.

"It's clear that something needs to be done in regard to this issue," Chad was saying. "Under my opponent's leadership, these problems have increased drastically."

Mike was given the opportunity for rebuttal and he laid out the statistics. Yes, there had been an escalation, but the number of arrests leading to conviction had also increased.

The moderator moved on to a question for Chad, asking what he thought the top priority should be for the next term for sheriff, other than public safety.

Chad gave one of his winning smiles and laid out his response. "Our children," he said. "Issues exist in the public school system and we need to make all the positive differences we can."

Anna mentally shook her head at Chad's canned answer to the question. He took the easy way out.

"Too bad Mike McBride is my brother's opponent." Chandra's platinum blonde hair swung forward as she leaned close to speak in Anna's ear. Anna caught the scent of Chandra's light floral perfume. "Mike is so gorgeous," Chandra said. "Beyond gorgeous." She sighed. "But he's the enemy."

Anna made a noncommittal response. How could she tell her friend that she thought Chad didn't stand a chance against Mike in the race or even in virility and looks?

With blond hair and blue eyes, Chad was good-looking and popular in his own right, but he was all politician. He was an attorney in Prescott and his family owned a good portion of the town. The Johnsons, for the most part, were well known and respected, with just a couple of bad apples in the bunch.

Anna shifted in her seat as Chad made a couple of disparaging remarks about Mike's term in office. She hated it when politicians played dirty, and she was certain Chad was that kind of politician. So far the race hadn't been too bad, but she could see it coming.

After Anna and her family moved to Prescott, she'd become good friends with Chandra, who was genuine and kind.

On the other hand was her twin. Whenever Chad had spoken with Anna, it had always seemed to her that he was preparing to run for office. At the time she hadn't realized he would be running for sheriff.

She looked down at her fashionable chunky black heels as she crossed her legs then tugged down her red dress that reached low on her thighs. She linked her fingers and rested her hands on her bare knee. Even though Chad came off as having a pleasing personality, she knew it was something he had worked hard to cultivate. He had a politician's polish and presence, and Anna wondered how far that would take him.

Unlike Mike, who had been a decorated officer with the Prescott Police Department, Chad was an attorney with no law enforcement experience. However, in Arizona, having that kind of experience wasn't required. It was archaic. All that was necessary for the individual running was that he or she was a legal Arizona resident and resided in the county for which they wanted to be sheriff. That was it. No job application, background check, criminal history check, or psychological examination was required. After being elected, they weren't even given job evaluations like other county employees.

Anna mentally shook her head. The sheriff wielded a great deal of power in the county and was responsible for enforcing the law and running the county jails, along with a great deal of responsibility beyond. That included managing a budget in the millions. With respect to requirements for running for sheriff, Arizona was a bit of a backward state.

"What is your position on illegal immigration?" the moderator asked Chad.

Anna froze. Ice seemed to chill her spine as Chad looked directly at her. The eye contact only lasted a moment but it felt as if her heart had stopped. She felt Chandra stiffen beside her.

Chad continued speaking, but Anna could barely hear him because of the buzzing in her ears. She caught a few words including "tougher stand on illegal immigration," and "crack down on undocumented aliens in Yavapai County."

She had known the subject would come up. It was an important topic on both parties' platforms, and to the people. But having Chad look at her and meet her gaze caused a sickening sensation to twist her belly.

Does he know? She glanced at Chandra who was watching Chad. *Did Chandra tell him?* It seemed as though Chandra was making a point of focusing on Chad. She looked...angry. Had Chandra let something slip accidentally? She wasn't the kind of person to do that knowingly.

Anna was so wrapped up in her thoughts that she didn't hear Mike's response to the question on illegal immigration. She was just grateful he hadn't looked at her. Not that he had any reason to—she'd never even met the sheriff.

When the moderator moved on to a different topic, Anna tried to relax. She knew that with the way things were, she'd never be able to let her guard down. Ever. It just wasn't possible.

Chandra reached over and squeezed her hand. Anna met her gaze. Her friend said nothing, but her friendship and support were clear. If Chad had learned Anna's secret, then it either hadn't been through Chandra or it had been inadvertent.

Anna gave Chandra a little smile before she turned back to the debate that had finally ended.

"Come on," Chandra said. "I told Chad I'd meet him after the debate."

The last thing Anna wanted to do was face Chad, but she forced a smile. "Sure. Let's go."

Both candidates left the stage and Anna hooked her purse over her shoulder and followed Chandra backstage to see her brother. Anna lost Chandra as they wended their way through the crowded area and Anna stopped and frowned as she tried to look past shoulders. At five-one, Anna had a bit of a height disadvantage.

A man's tall form stopped right in front of her. She looked up and caught her breath. Mike McBride. Looking right at her.

His presence filled the room in a way that made her feel as if no one else was there but the two of them. His aura was far more commanding than she'd ever noticed with Chad. He had seemed larger than life on stage, and in person his personality was magnetic. She couldn't take her eyes off him.

Mike held out his hand. "I don't believe we've met. I'm Mike McBride."

She took his hand and stilled. The heat that traveled through her was like magic. It tingled through her as if she had the power now to cast a spell. She swallowed and spoke hesitantly, which was so unlike her. "I'm Anna. Anna Batista."

"A pleasure to meet you, Anna." He gave a sexy smile that melted her. The smile was nothing like what she'd seen from him before when he'd spoken to TV cameras or during the debate. It was as if this one was made just for her.

Then it hit her. What if he'd learned her secret? Was that why he was talking with her? To learn more?

"Nice to meet you, too." She managed to draw her hand away from his but couldn't seem to move away from him to go find Chandra.

"I saw you standing here," he said with ease. "You look a little lost."

His charm had her completely off balance. "I lost my friend in the crowd." She pushed long dark strands from her face. "I'm sure I'll find her, though." *All I have to do is find your opponent.*

"Can I help?" Mike asked.

Now that could be awkward. She shook her head. "I can find her."

Still smiling, he said, "I haven't seen you around before. If I had, I would have noticed."

He didn't seem anxious to let her go on her way. To tell the truth, she didn't want to. She found herself craving his nearness, wanting to get closer to him.

"This is my first debate." She smiled. "You were great up there."

"Thank you." His brown eyes studied her. "Are you from Prescott?"

She shook her head. "Not originally."

"Where did you come from before?" he asked.

She tried to remain casual. "The southern part of the state. Bisbee area."

"Nice place, Bisbee." He hooked his thumbs in his jeans' pockets. "Been a while since I've been. I usually stay at the Copper Queen Hotel."

"It is a great town and there's so much history." She probably sounded inane as she tried to think of something to say. "You're a Prescott native, aren't you?"

He gave a nod. "Born and raised."

It didn't surprise her that he wasn't trying to sell himself to her as a candidate. He had a confidence about him and genuine to the point that she couldn't imagine him putting on airs or lying, for that matter. No, definitely not a real politician. She knew in her heart that he ran for office because he cared about the county and its residents.

She found herself wanting to be closer to him, wanting to get to know him.

But that would be a bad idea. A real bad idea, and it had nothing to do with her best friend's brother being Mike's opponent.

Mike studied Anna and sized her up. She was beautiful and all of five-one if he guessed correctly, and he was usually right on the mark. Soft brown curls fell around her heart-shaped face past her shoulders and her perfume was intriguing, inviting. Her dark brown eyes were wide and had an innocent quality to them, yet a strength that told him she stood up for what she believed in. She might be petite but he'd bet she was a fireball beneath all the softness.

And damn but she drew him in, made him want to get closer to her.

At the same time he sensed she was holding back something… An emotion, a circumstance… Something was beneath that calm, beautiful surface. He had a keen ability to size up people and he had a feeling that there was more to Anna Batista than what met the eye.

It was the first time in a long time that he'd been so attracted to a woman that he wanted to get to know her better, to find out what made her tick.

"I'm headed out to get something to eat at the Hummingbird." He studied her dark eyes. "Would you like to join me?"

A surprised look flashed across her honey-brown features and her lips parted. For the briefest moment she hesitated. From her expression he thought she would say yes, but instead she looked apologetic and said, "I'm sorry but I can't."

He gave a slow nod and pulled a business card out of his shirt pocket and a pen from inside the leather jacket that he'd put on over his uniform. He wrote his number on the back and handed it to her with the handwritten side up. "If you'd like to get together sometime, here's my card. That's my personal cell number."

Again she looked like he'd caught her off-guard. "Okay." She took the card from him in her small fingers and tucked it into a purse that hung to her hip. "Have a nice dinner."

He smiled. "Perhaps another night, Anna." He liked the way her name tasted on his tongue as he said it. "I hope you'll give me a call."

"Thank you for inviting me." She smiled but he could see a hint of wariness in her eyes. "Good luck in the race."

Her response was a little disappointing. Maybe she'd have a change of heart and would give him a call.

"I'd best be going." He touched his fingers to the brim of his hat. "Have a good night."

"Good night," she said. Did she look a little disappointed?

He gave her a nod and a smile before heading toward the back way, his thoughts staying on the beautiful woman. His mind ached to turn and watch her as she moved through the crowd.

"Great job." Jack McBride slapped Mike on the back as he came up from behind. Mike stopped and Jack flashed a grin. "I'd say you kicked Johnson's ass."

Mike's cousin, Jack, was lean but all muscle and his features were angular. He had a perpetual five-o'clock shadow that gave him a tough, weathered look. He was a rancher like most of the McBrides were, and he had a nice spread with over one hundred fifty head of cattle.

"It was a good debate," Mike said. And it had been, despite the fact that Mike's opponent was a rival from his youth. Mike hooked his thumbs in his front pockets as he looked at his cousin. "Don't know about kicking his ass."

"You sure as hell did." Jack raised his western hat and pushed his hand through his dark hair before settling the hat back on his head. "Johnson doesn't belong in office. He doesn't know what the hell he's doing. You, on the other hand, are the best damn sheriff we've had as far back as I can remember."

With his thumbs in his pockets, Mike rocked back on his heels. "Are you going to be at John and Hollie's wedding?"

"Wouldn't miss it," Jack said with a nod. "Never thought I'd see John marry."

"Yeah, it's hard to believe he's tying the knot." Mike thought about his brother and the woman who captured his heart. "John found himself a good woman in Hollie."

"All of your brothers ended up with fine women," Jack said. "Can't say you'll see me settling down in a hurry."

Mike thought about his own confirmed bachelorhood, then thought of Anna. He shook his head. "I make it a policy to never say never."

Jack clapped his hand on Mike's shoulder. "I have a gut feeling you'll be next."

Mike's lips quirked into a smile. "I'm headed to the Hummingbird for a bite to eat. You up for dinner?"

"Hell, yes," Jack said. "As long as they've got plenty of their famous peach pie."

"I'll bet they do." Mike started once again toward the back door leading from the auditorium.

Jack fell into step beside him. "Then let's get the hell out of here."

Hair at Mike's nape prickled. It felt as if someone was watching him intently. He casually glanced over his shoulder and met Anna Batista's gaze. A pretty blush tinged her cheeks and she quickly looked away.

With a grin, Mike stepped into the night with his cousin. Just maybe he'd caught Anna's attention after all. He wasn't sure yet just how, but some way he *would* get to know the beautiful woman, and sooner rather than later.

Chapter 2

Anna's cheeks burned as she looked away from the gaze of the man who'd captured her attention so thoroughly.

Mike McBride had just asked her out.

And she'd said no.

When Mike looked away and headed out the rear exit, Anna covertly watched his retreating form. His shoulders were broad, his ass and athletic thighs so very fine. His Stetson only added to his sexiness.

She swallowed, disappointment making her stomach feel heavy. She'd wanted to say yes so badly. The fact that he was her best friend's brother's enemy had kept her from accepting his invitation to dinner—she couldn't get into a relationship with the sheriff and not upset her friend. Chandra was so close to her twin brother.

Of course Mike had only asked Anna out to eat, so what was she worried about? That didn't mean he was interested in dating her.

But she'd seen it in his eyes. He'd pretty much made it clear he was interested. Why else would he ask her? It certainly couldn't be for her vote—a politician didn't take an average citizen out just to get her vote.

A thought came to her. Why shouldn't she go out with Mike? Maybe she could meet him for drinks. Yes, she'd call him and tell him she'd have a drink or two with him.

Mind made up, she straightened her bearing and looked once again for Chandra.

"Anna." A man's voice had her whirling around. *Chad.*

"Hi, Chad." She gave him a smile but had a hard time putting warmth behind it. "Good debate." Feeling nervous, she looked over her shoulder. "Where's Chandra?"

"She's talking with one of my aides." Chad gave Anna a practiced smile. "I saw you with my opponent. McBride gave you his card."

Something in his eyes told her that what he was going to say next wasn't good. "Yes." She gave him a bright smile. "You politicians like to score points with your voters."

He didn't blink. "McBride wrote his number on the back of his card."

"How do you know that?" she asked before she could stop herself.

"Speculation." Chad studied her. "You just confirmed it."

Her cheeks felt warm. "Like I said, politicians—"

He cut her off. "Don't play it down, Anna. I could see he's interested in you."

Her skin tingled, but this time it was from irritation. "What do you want, Chad?"

He gave her a politician's smile. "Just making sure I haven't lost you to the other side."

"Of course not." She looked past Chad and spotted Chandra. "I've got to meet up with your sister. See you."

Chad gave a smile and a nod. But somehow she felt like clammy fingers crawled along her spine. He had to know her secret and he was just playing with her, waiting for the right time to talk with her about it.

She waved at Chandra, catching her friend's attention. Without a backward glance at Chad, Anna worked her way toward Chandra who had just finished talking with a young man, who must have been one of the aides that Chad had mentioned. Chandra started toward Anna and they met up halfway.

"Where have you been?" Chandra asked. "You disappeared."

"Lost you in the crowd." Anna shrugged. "Got waylaid and then escaped and made it here."

With a laugh, Chandra said, "By who?"

Anna felt a moment's discomfort. "Your brother for one. He made it clear he wants my vote."

Chandra laughed. "That's my brother."

"Chandra," A female voice interrupted and Anna turned and saw that it was Leigh Monroe. Leigh caught sight of Anna and said as she reached them, "Hi, Anna."

"Haven't seen you around for a while," Anna said. "What's up?"

Leigh hesitated.

"Leigh broke up with her boyfriend again not long after I broke up with Neal," Chandra said. "They split before last Christmas, got together again, then just broke up a few days ago."

Anna reached out and touched Leigh's arm. "I'm sorry."

"It's all good." Leigh's throat worked and it looked as if she wanted nothing better than to change the subject. "We—we're just friends now."

"Leigh and I are going to Jo-Jo's to check out the guys," Chandra said. "Want to join us?"

Anna had the feeling that Leigh and Chandra were going to be talking more about the men who had broken their hearts recently than checking out the men, and she didn't want to interrupt. She also thought about her decision to call Mike. He was the only man she wanted to check out right now.

"I'll take a rain check," Anna said. "Where are you parked?" she asked Chandra.

"Out back." Chandra pointed toward the rear exit.

"I'm in front of the auditorium." Anna jerked her thumb in that direction and took a couple of steps back as she spoke. "I'll call you." To Leigh she added, "See you later, Leigh."

The two women waved and Anna waved back before heading out into the auditorium. As she walked, she pulled her cell phone out of her purse along with Mike's business card, and then punched his number into her phone. After another deep breath, she raised the phone to her ear.

A beat later, Mike's deep voice came on the line. "Sheriff McBride."

"Hi, Sheriff." Anna swallowed as butterflies batted around in her belly. "This is Anna Batista. We just met."

"Hi, Anna." He had a smile in his voice. "Taking me up on dinner?"

"Why don't we have a drink?" She would play it cool. "I can meet you at Nectars."

"That would be fine," he said. "What time?"

She gripped her phone tightly. "How about eight?"

"Perfect," he said. "I'll see you then, Anna."

"See you," she said before she disconnected the call.

Her hand gripped the strap of her purse until it ached. When she walked down the steps from the stage to the auditorium, she saw that the auditorium was mostly deserted now. She hurried up an aisle and out the front entrance.

Now she had two hours to kill and she had no idea what to do with the time. She settled on going shopping. It was a Wednesday and still early enough that plenty of stores would still be open.

The air was cool when she stepped out through the double doors. Fortunately she'd had a good parking place, so she reached her Honda in no time. She unlocked the car and grabbed a sweater from the backseat and slipped it on.

After she got into her car, she called her aunt to tell her she wouldn't be home for dinner then started the vehicle. Which store should she start off with? She decided to check out the sales at her favorite dress boutique. She put her car into gear and headed to the store.

Right now she was feeling unsettled. The feeling likely had something to do with Chad looking right at her when he was talking about illegal immigration.

Shopping was a comfort and would get her mind off of the subject. Like some people ate or smoked for comfort, she shopped. She had a closet full of shoes and stylish clothing. She usually bought things on sale—she was a smart shopper—but she probably spent more than she should.

Okay, truth was that she did buy more than she should, but she only bought what she could afford.

She had a great reputation as an event planner and was paid well. She worked not only in Prescott and Flagstaff, but traveled to parts of the Phoenix metro area. Her work frequently took her out of town, but she didn't mind the travel and she loved planning and executing the events. Weddings were her bread and butter, but birthdays, parties, conventions, and trade shows also brought in a good income.

Her favorite boutique was open like she'd thought and she found a parking spot directly in front of it. Devora Snow was dressing a mannequin as Anna walked into the store. Bells jangled as she entered.

"Anna." Devora smiled. Blue and purple streaks of color in her dark blonde hair glimmered in the shop's lighting. "What are you up to?"

"Hi, Dev." Anna returned the smile. "I'm here to check your sale rack, of course."

"Of course." Devora flashed a grin as she moved away from the mannequin to the sale rack. "And I have just the dress for you. It's your size and a petite."

In moments Anna was trying on a stunning black dress that hugged her curves and rose high on her thighs. She came out of the changing room to model the dress for Devora.

"Beautiful." Devora clapped her hands and held them to her breastbone. "It was made for you, Anna."

Anna turned around in front of the full-length mirror and looked over her shoulder to see how the dress looked from the back. It did fit her well. She imagined wearing the dress while out on a date with Mike and had to hold back a frown. She liked the thought of dating Mike, but what about Chandra? She loved her friend to death, but Chandra was staunchly loyal to Chad.

Devora cocked her head to the side. "What's wrong?"

"Nothing." Anna gave a bright smile. "I'll take the dress. Got any new shoes that would go with this dress?"

"Right this way." Devora gestured for Anna to follow her.

Anna padded across the carpeted floor as she followed Devora to the boutique's shoe section. "Those are adorable." Anna went straight to a pair of black heels with a single strap in front that went up the top of the foot to an ankle strap. The straps sparkled with crystals. "Freaking awesome."

Devora laughed. "I thought of you when they came in."

"You know me so well it's scary." Anna picked up one of the heels. "I'm guessing you have them in my size?"

"One pair, just for you." Devora gave a nod toward the back room. "I'll get them now and you can try them on."

If they fit, Anna knew she'd be going home with at least a stunning new dress and killer pair of heels. Of course she'd have to check out jewelry, too.

I'm a junkie, she thought as she held up the shoe. *Gotta have my fix.*

Devora returned, carrying a bright pink box, and Anna sat on the nearby padded bench and slipped on the heels. She walked around in them, trying them out, and looking at them in the full-length mirror. The shoes fit perfectly and looked just as good with the dress as Anna had thought they would.

She still had time to kill so she tried on more dresses and more shoes. She ended up with the first dress and shoes, a pair of black slacks, and a black sweater with a silky black camisole. She tended to where a lot of black. She also found jewelry to go along with each outfit she'd purchased.

Over an hour after entering the store, Anna carried her purchases to the door. With a look over her shoulder, Anna said, "See you, Devora."

Devora gave a wave. "Oh, I'd say within a week."

"Yes, you know me far too well." Anna looked at her packages and gave a rueful shake of her head. "See you then."

Devora grinned and the bells at the top of the door jangled as Anna let herself out into the night.

CHAPTER 3

Shopping had been fun. Anna found shopping to be a nice escape from reality, like a good book was. Almost. She rationalized her purchases as important for her career, but truth was that she was a shopping addict, no two ways about it.

After stowing her packages in the back of her Honda, she climbed into the driver's seat, started the car, and headed to Nectars to meet Mike.

She parked a little way down the street, behind a black SUV. Her heart raced a little faster as she stepped out of her car and pulled on a light wrap. She hitched her purse up on her shoulder and locked the vehicle before dropping her keys into an inner pocket of the purse. She took a deep breath, shored up her courage and her resolve, and headed toward the entrance of the upscale bar.

Nectars was next to the Hummingbird restaurant, where Mike had said he was having dinner. The owners of the Hummingbird also owned Nectars.

Darkness had settled over the town and Anna shivered. It was fall and cool out, especially in the evenings. She couldn't complain though, the weather was gorgeous here compared to other states where it was already snowing.

Her courage faltered. What was she doing, meeting the sheriff for drinks? She stopped on the sidewalk for a moment and closed her eyes.

Why not? she asked herself. *He's a great guy.* When she opened her eyes again, she raised her chin and walked into the bar.

The interior was dim and she blinked a few times to get used to it. She let her gaze drift over the crowd before she spotted Mike, who was sitting at a high top and talking with a man Anna didn't recognize. Mike had changed out of his uniform and was wearing a western-style blazer shirt with jeans and black boots. She wondered if he kept a change of clothes in his vehicle or if he'd gone home to change. Did he live in town or out? She mentally shook her head. Why did she care?

Mike glanced her way, smiled, and got to his feet. She straightened her shoulders and started toward Mike and the other man, butterflies tickling her belly. The sheriff was so damned handsome, with a rugged, larger-than-life presence. The man next to him wasn't half bad at all, but as far as she was concerned, Mike was the best-looking man in the bar.

When she reached the table, Mike greeted her with a smile and took her hand between his. She liked the way it felt when he touched her—it made her feel pleasantly warm all over. He was at least a foot taller than her, but he didn't make her feel small at all. She felt comfortable with him.

He gave her hand a squeeze before releasing her. He lightly touched her back as he turned to the other man. "Jayson, this is Anna Batista." He turned to Anna. "Anna, this is one of my cousins, Jayson McBride. You may have seen his twin at the debate."

"I thought you looked familiar." Anna held out her hand and smiled at Jayson. "Great to meet you."

"Likewise." Jayson took her hand in a firm grip then released her. He turned to Mike. "I best be going."

"Don't leave on my account," Anna said.

"I need to get back to the ranch. Just got a call that one of my fences is down." Jayson nodded to Mike. "See you Sunday when I bring over that mare."

"You bet," Mike said.

Jayson touched the brim of his hat as he met Anna's gaze. "Hope to see you around."

She smiled. "Have a good evening."

He gave another nod then turned and headed out the door.

Anna faced Mike.

"I hope you don't mind sitting at a high top." Mike pulled out a chair and took her hand as he helped her into her seat.

"This is perfect." She settled in and hooked the strap of her purse on one side of her straight-backed chair. She slid out of her wrap and let it drape over the back of the seat beside her.

When Mike was seated in the chair on the opposite side of the table, he rested one forearm on the tabletop. Before either of them could say anything, a pretty server with bouncy blonde curls and a huge bust came up to the table. She was holding a tray with empty beer bottles and glasses in one hand.

The server smiled at Mike as she set a cocktail napkin in front of Anna. "What would you like to drink, sweetie?" she asked Anna.

"The house Chardonnay," Anna replied.

"Another Blue Moon?" the server asked Mike.

"Yes." He gave a nod. "Thanks, Rosie."

"Love your shoes," Rosie said to Anna with a smile, then glanced at Mike. "One Blue Moon and the house Chardonnay coming up."

Anna smiled as Rosie headed off to the bar with the tray of empties held high. Anna turned and met Mike's gaze. He was studying her as if he could see into the depths of her soul. As if he could learn every secret she held tightly to her heart.

Her stomach bottomed out. She shouldn't be meeting with the sheriff, of all people. What had she been thinking? She hadn't been thinking, that was the problem. What if he learned her secret?

Mike held her gaze. "You are a beautiful woman, Anna."

Heat crept into her cheeks. "Thank you."

"I'm glad you called because I'd like to get to know you." His eyes were chocolate brown, so very beautiful, as he studied her. "What do you do for a living?"

"I'm an event planner." She could handle this topic. "I plan events locally as well as in Flag and Phoenix."

He gave a slow nod. "Do you have any kids? Any exes in the wings?"

"Not really." She shook her head, her long, dark brown hair sliding over her shoulders. "No kids, never married, and no recent breakups or heartbreaks."

"But there have been heartbreaks," he said.

"It's been a couple of years." She clenched her fingers in her lap. "I don't believe in regrets over past relationships." She gave a light shrug. "Things are meant to happen for a reason and everything that happens is a stepping stone to what is meant to be."

"I like the way you look at things," he said. "You're a positive individual."

Most of the time, she thought. "Tell me about you."

"My life's an open book." He gave a little grin. "Part of being an elected official."

She tilted her head to the side. "Isn't that hard? People knowing almost everything about you?"

"Almost is a key word." He leaned back as Rosie arrived and set drinks in front of them.

"Anything off the menu?" Rosie asked as she looked from Mike to Anna and back.

"Did you eat dinner?" Mike asked Anna.

She shook her head. "I'm fine, though."

"I had a light dinner," he said. "Why don't we get the appetizer sampler?"

"Okay," she said. "I could go for a little something."

Rosie left and Anna took a sip of wine before she turned her attention back to Mike. "So, do you have any kids or exes?"

"Not a one." He shook his head. "I'd like a couple, though." He gave a quick grin. "I'd like a couple of kids, that is." She thought she saw a flicker of more darkness in his eyes as he added, "Exes I do have, and I don't need any more of those."

A shiver ran down her spine. If she and Mike did get together, she might end up being one of those exes and cause darkness where there should only be light. There would be no way they could get into a relationship and him not find out eventually.

She really needed to get out of here.

What would it hurt to have a drink with this hot, sexy sheriff?

Mike was studying her again, looking as if he could read her thoughts. She gave him a bright smile. "How is your campaign going, Sheriff?"

"Call me Mike." A smile was in his eyes as he set down his beer bottle. "As for my campaign, I think it could use a boost."

She tilted her head to the side. "In what way?"

"I'm not much of a politician. I'd rather be out doing my job." He looked thoughtful. "As much as I'm not crazy about campaigning, I need to get in touch with certain parts of the community."

"What about doing a few meet and greets?" Her mind went through all of the possibilities she could think of and she laid out a few ideas for places he could visit and get in contact with the community. "I'd bet the papers would love more interviews as well."

"They might love to interview me, but that's one of my least favorite things." He shook his head as he raised his beer bottle. "Of course, you're probably right."

Mike seemed keenly interested in her suggestions and asked her opinion on various aspects of his campaign.

"What about Halloween?" she asked. "You could do some safety promo for the kids in the schools."

He considered it. "I like that idea." He took a swig of his beer and set the bottle down. "Halloween's always been a fun time for my family. I have an aunt who throws one hell of a party every year for the family, especially for the kids." He shook his head. "And more kids keep sprouting up, as busy as this bunch has been."

"How about a little media coverage for the party?" Anna tapped her manicured nails on the tabletop as she thought about it. "It would show that you might not be married, but you're still a family man."

"I'm not sure about bringing the family into it, but I think you're on to something." He gave a grin that was so sexy it made her skin tingle. "I'll be happy to put you to work in PR if you're willing to join my campaign."

She looked at him in surprise. "You're offering me a job?"

"Part-time if you're available." He gave a nod. "For what's left of the campaign."

Without really thinking about it, she said, "I'd love to." She set her wine glass down and moved her hands to her lap. "I like to keep busy. I have a bit of a lull in my business right now. I'll be swamped come November and December, after the election. Lots of Christmas parties and employer functions on the calendar."

"Great." He smiled. "Welcome aboard."

Rosie arrived with the huge appetizer sample that included nachos, loaded potato skins, deep-fried and battered mozzarella cheese sticks, mushrooms and zucchini.

"Wow. This will be my indulgence for the week," Anna said to Mike with a laugh.

He flashed her another grin. "Nothing like bar food to clog your arteries."

Anna was grateful to be able to eat and let Mike do the talking for a while. She knew he'd ordered the platter for her since she hadn't eaten dinner, but was glad that he ate a good amount. It was a hell of a lot of food.

To keep from talking too much about her own life, she asked him about his family and he shared things about his parents with her as well as stories about his brothers. She enjoyed listening to him, loved the sound of his voice. It mesmerized her, drew her in.

He told her that John was his brother by blood, and Reese and Garrett were his stepbrothers. Mike shared with her that he was as close to his stepbrothers as he was with his blood brother. All four of them were in some type of law enforcement. John was a police lieutenant with the Prescott Police Department but after his wedding would be retiring to ranch. Reese was a detective at the PPD as was his wife. Garrett was a PI with his own agency and his wife owned the local bakery.

Anna put her elbow on the table and her chin on her hand. "I don't know which family is larger. The Johnsons or the McBrides."

Mike gave a low laugh. "Now that's a good question."

"From what I understand, the McBrides own most of the ranchland in the Prescott Valley," Anna said. "And the Johnsons own a big chunk of Prescott itself."

"There's some truth to that," Mike said. "But the Valley is so damned big that what the McBrides own is only a portion of what's available out there. And the town has grown so much that the Johnsons' share has gotten a good deal smaller."

Anna nodded, thinking of Chad. He wore the mantle of being a Johnson like a king, whereas Mike seemed to be more humble. Even though she knew no love was lost between Mike and Chad, in Mike's words and deeds he treated Chad with respect. She couldn't say the same for Chad. She'd heard him tear down Mike more than once.

When Anna had eaten her fill, she pushed aside her appetizer plate and her eyes met Mike's. She felt the need to fill the gap in conversation, but before she could say anything, he said, "I've been doing all the talking. Why don't you tell me a little more about you and your family?"

Her scalp prickled. What the hell was she doing here? In her situation, she didn't belong here and she shouldn't be talking about her family. She'd been so attracted to Mike that she hadn't been thinking clearly. She'd been letting her heart do all the thinking, ignoring her brain.

It wouldn't hurt to tell him a little. "I live with my Aunt Maria, Uncle Tito, and two young cousins, Josie and Pablo. They are five and eight and good kids." She smiled. "I adore them all."

"Did they come with you from Bisbee?" Mike asked.

Anna shifted on her seat. "Yes." To avoid talking any further about her family, she reached out to the appetizer tray and dipped her finger into the nacho cheese sauce. She brought her finger to her lips and sucked the cheese off.

Mike's eyes seemed to go darker as he watched her and she felt suddenly trapped in his gaze. Her belly fluttered and her breath caught in her chest. She wondered if he was imagining what else she might do with her mouth and heat flushed over her as the image of such an erotic moment flashed through her mind.

She slowly drew her finger out of her mouth and tried to look away from him but couldn't. It was an endless gaze that seemed to last forever yet it had been but a few heartbeats.

Finally she forced her eyes from his and looked at some of the other patrons. Nectars catered to an eclectic crowd and it was a great place to people watch. A couple kissed in a corner while a cluster of young women laughed and giggled in a booth. Nearby, one cowboy in a group of four was telling the others about a rattlesnake he'd killed on his property that he said had been at least eleven feet long and weighed fifteen to twenty pounds. She was wondering if rattlesnakes really could get that big.

When she turned back to Mike, he gave her a quick grin. "That boy's telling a bit of a tall tale unless he's discovered a record-sized diamondback. At most they can reach as much as eight feet long and weigh up to ten pounds."

"That answers my question," she said with a return grin, grateful to be past the intimate moment they had just shared. Before he could ask her more questions about her life, she hurried to say, "I'd better be going. I have an event on Friday—a wedding—and I need to be on top of my game."

"I'll walk you out to your car." He signaled to Rosie who brought the check. Anna thought about offering to pay half, but knew inside that he wouldn't agree to it.

After he laid out cash for the drinks and appetizers with the bill, he got up from his seat. He helped Anna off of her stool and assisted her with her wrap. He was such the gentleman that it made her smile.

Several people waved or nodded to Mike and said, "Goodnight, Sheriff." She'd been enjoying herself so much that she'd started thinking of him as Mike and not as the sheriff anymore.

When they stepped out into the chill night, Anna hugged her wrap tighter around her. Mike shrugged out of his blazer and put it around her shoulders.

She looked at him with surprise. "You didn't have to do that. Now you'll be cold."

"I'm doing just fine," he said with a smile.

When they reached her car, she unlocked it with the remote and he opened the door for her. She looked up at him and her heart skipped a beat. He was looking at her with such intensity that it nearly took her breath away.

In that moment she wanted him to kiss her more than anything in the world. By the look in his eyes, he was thinking the same thing.

He rested one hand on the door, his other on the car, caging her in. His throat worked and he said, "Thank you for meeting me tonight. I enjoyed your company."

"I enjoyed yours, too." She mentally braced herself. Was he going to kiss her? Should she let him? God, how she wanted him to.

"Can I call you tomorrow?" he asked.

She nodded. "My mobile phone is the number I called you from."

"Great." He smiled. "When I call, you can let me know then if you're still interested in working for my campaign."

"Okay." She gripped the handle of her purse. "Thank you for the drink and appetizers."

Their eyes held and she just knew he was going to kiss her. And she wanted him to with everything she had.

He took a step back. "Good night, Anna."

A rush of disappointment shot through her. She didn't want the night to end, yet she'd been the one to tell him she had to leave.

Something flickered in his eyes and he reversed and closed what distance had been between them. He slid his fingers into her hair and cupped the back of her head, and put his other hand to the small of her back. He drew her body closer to his as he brought his mouth down on hers in a decisive movement.

He'd moved so quickly, he caught her off guard. Her lips parted. He took her in a thorough kiss, his mouth firm against her soft lips. She kissed him back, a sigh escaping her into his mouth.

With a low groan, he drew away and raised his head. He slid his fingers from her hair and ran his thumb over her lips slowly. "I shouldn't have done that." He studied her. "I should have asked."

She could barely think, much less talk. Still she got out the words that betrayed her. "I wanted you to."

"You'd better get on home now." He caressed her hair from where it lay across her cheek.

"Good night, Mike," she said softly. She started to climb into her car when she realized she was still wearing his blazer over her shoulders. She started to take it off. "Oh. Don't forget—"

He stilled her hands. "I'll get it from you next time I see you."

She gripped the blazer. "Are you sure?"

"It'll give me an excuse to see you again," he said with a searching look.

"You don't need an excuse," she said softly.

What am I saying beat at the back of her thoughts, but her stupid heart ignored her brain.

He smiled. "I'm going to wait until you're safely on your way."

She slid into the car, started it, and turned on the heater before looking up at him. "Good night, Mike."

He rested his hand on the door. "Good night, Anna." He shut the door firmly and it severed the connection that she'd felt between them. That connection had kept her warm and now she felt the chill air that hadn't been heated yet inside her car.

She glanced at him as he stood aside while she pulled her car from the curb. She looked in the rearview mirror one last time as she drove down the street to see him still standing, watching her drive away.

Dear God, what was she doing?

She shook her head and gripped the steering wheel. She was going to have to stop this before it went any further.

Her lips still tingled from his kiss and she put her fingertips against them. Without warning, the backs of her eyes started burning. What she wouldn't give for things to be different.

She moved her hand from her mouth and gripped the steering wheel. Wishing wasn't going to make any difference, but she had control over what would happen from this time on. She'd just have to tell Mike that she wasn't in a place in her life for a relationship at this time. Yes, that's what she would do.

For no reason at all she felt a sense of loss. She shook her head and pushed the feeling away. She didn't even know Mike so she was losing nothing.

Then why did her chest squeeze until her heart hurt?

Love at first sight or at first touch had never seemed possible until tonight. For her it had been at first kiss.

"That's impossible," she said aloud, her voice sounding raw. "It is not possible at all."

But her heart knew differently. Her only choice was to squash what her heart felt. She had to go with what her head knew she was supposed to do.

CHAPTER 4

All night, Anna's dreams had been filled with Mike. She tossed and turned, barely able to sleep. Her dreams had turned erotic, the kiss they'd shared becoming something far more intimate. She dreamt of his touch, of his body weighing hers down as he slid between her thighs…

In the morning her head ached and she felt as if she'd been crying even though she hadn't been. She pushed her fingers through her hair and was determined to get her head on straight.

When she got out of bed, she spotted his blazer lying over a chair in her room, moved toward the chair, and picked up the blazer. She brought it to her nose, inhaling Mike's scent.

Her stomach flip-flopped as she imagined having him wrapped around her instead of the blazer. She dropped it back on the chair as if it might burn her if she held it any longer.

After she'd showered and put on her makeup, she dressed in a pair of black slacks and a cream sweater, along with a pair of black ankle boots. When she was prepared to face the day, she wandered out of her bedroom. Before she even reached the kitchen, she caught the wonderful smell of chorizo and eggs and her stomach growled. She headed into the kitchen and saw her aunt preparing breakfast at the stove.

At five feet tall, Aunt Maria was an inch shorter than Anna. Maria had a full figure and her gray hair was pulled back into a tight bun. She wore an apron over her uniform and sturdy shoes.

"Good morning, Aunt Maria," Anna said in Spanish.

Her aunt still struggled with English and usually admonished Anna to speak in English to help her better learn the language. Anna's aunt and uncle had come to the U.S. from Mexico City. The children were born in the U.S.

Today when Maria looked over her shoulder, she responded in Spanish, "You look tired, my child."

"I'm fine." Anna switched to English as she opened the fridge and pulled out a carton of orange juice. "Where is everyone?"

"Of course your Uncle Tito left early for work with the landscaper." Maria enunciated each word clearly but with a strong accent. She picked up the frying pan and slid the chorizo and eggs onto a plate then added a folded homemade flour tortilla. "Your cousins are at school."

"It's that late?" Anna set the orange juice on the counter as she glanced at the clock. It was after nine. She took a glass out of a cabinet. "What are you doing here, fixing me breakfast?"

Maria got out a fork and a napkin. "Josephina called last night. Our first house cancelled," she said as she carried the plate of chorizo and eggs, as well as the fork and napkin, to the table. Maria worked for a house cleaning service.

Anna knew her aunt was disappointed at the loss of income and a twinge of guilt stabbed at Anna's belly for her shopping spree yesterday. Not that it would have made a difference in the household. Anna would have gladly paid all of the rent, utilities, and groceries, but her aunt and uncle were proud and insisted on paying half of everything. It hurt their pride deeply if they couldn't make their half and still send money to relatives in Mexico. Anna just felt guilty because she could afford so much and they had so little. But they wouldn't allow her to spend money on them.

Knowing that her aunt wouldn't be pleased at Anna's train of thought, she made herself smile and she said, "It looks and smells so good."

Maria pointed toward the breakfast table. "Sit."

Anna put the carton of juice back into the fridge and carried her glass to the table. She slid into a seat and held back a grin. "Yes, ma'am."

With a return smile, Maria set the plate in front of Anna along with a fork and a napkin. "You are right. It is good."

Anna set her glass on the table. "Is that menudo I smell, too?" Anna said as she picked up her fork.

"It will be ready for dinner." Maria untied her apron and pulled it over her head. "It is time for me to go. We have a house at nine-thirty." She hung the apron on a hook inside the pantry door before closing the door. "Tomorrow is an event, yes? A wedding?"

Anna swallowed the delicious bite of her breakfast. "Yes." In the past, she had offered her aunt and uncle various jobs to help at her events, but they considered that charity, too, so she'd learned not to ask them. "It's in Phoenix so I'll be leaving early."

Maria rested her hand on Anna's shoulder. "You're a good girl, our little Anna."

"Who are you calling little?" Anna grinned at her aunt. "Last I checked you were shorter than me."

Maria laughed and squeezed Anna's shoulder. "I will see you tonight."

"Would you like a ride to Josephina's?" Anna asked. "I can save this and eat it when I get back."

Maria took her house keys off of a hook and slipped them into her pocket. "You eat while it's still hot. I will walk. It does me good."

"See you later, Aunt Maria," Anna said fondly to her aunt.

Maria gave a smile and a nod and headed out of the kitchen to the living room and then out the front door. Josephina's home was a fifteen-minute walk from Anna's house, but Maria walked every day. She didn't have a driver's license much less a vehicle to drive. Uncle Tito drove their old pickup truck to work early in the mornings.

As Anna cleaned the breakfast dishes, she kept turning thoughts of last night over and over in her mind. What had she been *thinking*? This was her life, her reality. She couldn't date a sheriff and endanger the welfare of the ones she loved.

With new resolve, she shrugged into her jacket, grabbed her purse then headed out to her car. Before running errands, she needed to go to Chandra's home and see her friend for a few minutes. Anna had to tell Chandra that she'd gone out on a date with Mike before Chandra heard it from someone else.

Anna blew out her breath. She would let Chandra know that she didn't intend to see the sheriff again. It had been one night with a drink and appetizers, and that was it. Anna certainly wasn't going to let her friend know about the kiss.

The day was cool and overcast, the sky filled with dark gray clouds, and Anna wondered if it was going to rain. The drive to Chandra's house was only five minutes and Anna had her answer to her question as fat drops of rain splattered her windshield.

When she reached Chandra's home, she parked and hurried out of her car to the covered porch that ran the length of the front of the house. Her ankle boots thunked against wood as she headed up the steps.

Before she could press the doorbell, the door swung open. For a moment she couldn't tell who had opened the door because the screen was too dark to see through. Chad pushed open the screen door and gave her a smile that struck her as smarmy. He had a glint in his eyes that made her uncomfortable.

"Good morning, Anna," he said, the look in his eyes made her feel like he believed he shared a secret with her.

"Hi, Chad." She stepped into the house as he closed the door behind them.

She looked around the elegant living room with its rich wood flooring. The room was filled with antiques and a collection of Lladro figurines in a huge lighted curio with curved glass. The Johnsons were wealthy and it showed in everything they owned.

"Chandra should be downstairs in a few." Chad took a step closer to Anna. As he moved in closer, her only thought was that this wasn't going to be good.

"So you got up close and personal with Sheriff McBride last night," Chad said and Anna's skin prickled. "Kissing the enemy."

How did he know? "I'm not planning on seeing him again," she stated.

"You're not?" He raised his brows. "I think you need to reconsider."

She narrowed her brows. What game was he playing at? "I don't see that it's any of your business what I do." She tried to keep her voice even.

"But it is my business. I want you to get close to McBride." Chad's voice hardened but he kept it low. "I want you to get on the inside of his campaign. Not only can you get to him personally but you're also an event planner. You can volunteer for his campaign."

Her jaw dropped. "You want me to spy on the sheriff?"

"You either help me," Chad said in a dangerous tone, "or a call might just be made to the authorities."

She felt blood drain from her face. "You're blackmailing me?"

"Let's don't call it that." He gave his politician's smile. "Let's call it an incentive."

"You—you—" She'd been about to say *bastard*, but the look in his eyes had her clamping her mouth shut before she said, "What will Chandra think?"

Chad glanced over his shoulder and she looked past him to see Chandra coming down the stairs. He faced Anna again. "She's not to know."

"Chandra is my best friend." Anna stared at him with incredulity. "You expect me to go over to your political enemy without her knowing why I would choose the sheriff over you?"

"You'd better believe it," Chad said. "Tell her nothing."

"How would I explain it to her?" Anna asked. "If I even agree to this?"

"You will agree, or else." His words had a finality to them. "You'll think of something to tell Chandra." He smirked. "Just tell her the sheriff asked you out and he makes you hot enough to fuck him."

The heat that flushed through Anna this time felt like it was burning her from the inside out. "You sonofabitch," she hissed, barely able to keep her voice down or her hand from slapping his face.

"You'd better watch it," Chad cautioned. "You never know how word can get to the authorities."

She clenched and unclenched her hands. With a smile that she now found sickening rather than attractive, he turned and headed into the Johnsons' extensive library.

"What's wrong?" Chandra's voice brought Anna's attention around to her friend.

"Wrong?" Anna tried to school her features. "Nothing's wrong."

Chandra shook her head, her platinum blonde hair swinging above her shoulders. "You can't fool me, sweetheart."

Anna tried to think fast. She had no choice but to go along with Chad's blackmail. She took a deep breath. "I was attempting to think of a way to tell you that I had drinks with Sheriff McBride last night."

Chandra blinked. "You went on a date with him?"

"Yes." Anna dug the card out of her purse and showed the back to Chandra. "He gave me his personal cell phone number yesterday and I called him."

Chandra's eyes had widened. "And you're planning on seeing him again?"

Anna hesitated and then jumped into the role. "Yes. He said he wants to see me again and I'm going to go out with him. He's nice, and like you said, he is gorgeous."

"You'd go out with Chad's opponent?" Chandra's features were tinged with pink. "How long have you known me? How long have you known Chad?"

Anna felt close to tears. "I'm sorry." Damn Chad for putting her in this position.

Chandra straightened her spine. "Go ahead and date the sheriff. Just don't expect me to give you my blessing."

"Chandra," Anna said in a pleading voice.

Her face flushed with color, Chandra stepped back. "I've got things to do."

Anna opened her mouth to tell Chandra to wait, but her friend turned and marched toward her kitchen then disappeared through the archway. She didn't stop to look back once.

Chad returned to the living room from the library, carrying a book. Even though his lips didn't show it, a smile was in his eyes. "See you around, Anna."

Tears burned at the backs of Anna's eyes, but she tilted her chin up and refused to cry. *Damn you, Chad Johnson.* Damn *you.*

Spine rigid, she turned her back on him and walked out of the house.

Anger burned through her as she headed down the stairs and then down the sidewalk to her car, not caring about the raindrops pelting her. She jerked the door open and slid into the driver's seat before slamming the door shut.

She gripped the steering wheel so tightly that her hands ached as water trickled down the side of her face. Drops splattered her windshield, blurring her view of the house.

That bastard. She started her vehicle then sat for a long moment with the rain coming down and her car running, while different scenarios played through her mind. The problem was that all but one scenario ended badly. The one that didn't was the only acceptable option—she had to go along with Chad's blackmail.

Of course her only choice was not really a choice, and she could hurt other people in the process, so it could end badly, too. Her best friend was already upset and felt like Anna was a traitor. What if Anna did get close to Mike and hurt him, too?

She could sit in her car, fuming over Chad's blackmail, or she could go about her day and plan on seeing Mike again.

With her jaw clenched, she flipped on her windshield wipers. The car's tires spun in the crushed white rock in front of the Johnson house as she backed up. Her car shot forward as she put it in drive. With her jaw set, she headed toward her first stop. All she could do was go on with her day.

And plan on spying on Mike.

* * * * *

"Freddy Victors was murdered in prison?" Mike turned the news over in his mind as he listened to his brother.

"We think Jesus Perez ordered the hit in retaliation for his brother's murder and the killings of two of his top men," John said. "Can't say the world isn't better off without Freddy."

John had good reason not to mourn Freddy Victors. The man had set up John's fiancée for a murder she didn't commit, and Freddy had come close to killing her, too.

"Perez's foothold in the drug trade is firmer than it's ever been," John added

"That was pretty much established when Freddy was arrested and convicted of murder." Mike blew out his breath as he stared out the internal window of the Yavapai County Sheriff's Office, YCSO, his gaze drifting over his assistant and other staff members.

"Yep," John said. "Freddy still had men who we believe he was able to communicate with from prison. That certainly won't be the case now."

Mike shifted in his office chair. "Any new intel on Perez?"

"No more than we discussed the last time," John said. "He's still a suspect in smuggling illegal immigrants into the area as well as drugs."

"Let me know if you get anymore and I'll do the same," Mike said.

"You've got it," John said before he disconnected the call.

Mike hung up his office phone and his thoughts turned to Anna. Damn but he hadn't been able to get her off his mind since last night. His gut tightened. That kiss—she'd tasted sweet as he'd inhaled her scent and felt her petite body close to his.

It had been some time since he'd been with a woman, but old hurts had healed and he was ready for a relationship with the right woman. Anna could be the one.

Whatever the case, he knew he had to see her again. He unholstered his mobile phone and brought up the number she'd given him last night. He felt like a teenager as he dialed the number, hoping she'd pick up.

"This is Anna," she answered in her sexy voice.

Mike smiled. "How's your day going?"

"Hi, Sheriff—Mike." She sounded hesitant. "It's going well." She sounded a little off, not as warm as she had been last night.

"If this isn't a good time," Mike said, "I can call you later."

"Oh." Her voice changed so that it was more upbeat. "Now is good."

"Thanks for meeting me last night." He leaned back in his office chair. "I enjoyed your company."

"I liked spending time with you, too." She had a smile in her voice.

"Are you free sometime this weekend?" He gripped his phone. "You mentioned an event on Friday. Does Saturday or Sunday work?"

In his mind he could picture the delicate smile on her heart-shaped face, her long dark hair falling down her back and over her shoulders. "Yes, I have a wedding in Phoenix on Friday. The rest of the weekend is clear."

"How about Saturday?" he asked.

"I'm free any time that day," she said.

He felt unusually pleased, in a way he hadn't felt with another woman. "I'll pick you up at noon."

A smile was in her voice. "Are you going to give me a clue about where we're going?"

He gave a low chuckle. "You might want to wear jeans and comfortable shoes."

She laughed. "I'll be ready and I'll bring your blazer." After she gave him her address, there was another hesitation before she said, "If you'd still like me to work with you on your campaign, my schedule frees up on Monday."

"Perfect." His desk phone rang. "I've got a call to take. I'll see you Saturday."

"See you," she echoed.

He couldn't help smiling as he disconnected the call and reached for his desk phone.

CHAPTER 5

For a long moment Anna stared up at the ceiling when she woke late Saturday morning. Her head ached from exhaustion and her belly twisted with both excitement and worry. The exhaustion came from yesterday's event in Phoenix, the excitement to do with her date with Mike today—and worry about Chad's blackmail and her family's safety.

The wedding had been a real challenge with the mother of the bride, Mrs. Smyth, finding fault in everything and anything to do with the event. Mrs. Smyth had fluttered around exclaiming how the flowers weren't the exact shade of pink she'd wanted; the wedding bouquet wasn't big enough; the cake wasn't cream filled but raspberry filled—even though Anna knew the mother had ordered the raspberry filled white cake; the chairs weren't set up exactly right; the wedding photographer took too long; the music wasn't to her taste; she hadn't liked the food, and the list went on.

Anna scooted up in bed and stretched while letting out a yawn. She had, of course, been patient with Mrs. Smyth. With the exception of the fussy mother, the wedding truly had gone on without a hitch. Mrs. Smyth would have complained about everything, no matter how perfect it might be. The wedding *would* have been perfect without the complaining woman. But from experience, Anna was no stranger to brides' mothers. Anna was almost always complimented for the events she pulled off, thanked for her work, and well tipped.

Then there were people like Mrs. Smyth. In this case Mr. Smyth had apologized for his wife and had given a handsome tip "for having to put up with the woman," as he put it.

Anna slid out of bed and turned her thoughts to today. She couldn't help the excited little thrill in her belly at the prospect of spending time with Mike. Not only was he a gorgeous cowboy, but he was intelligent, interesting to talk with, and had an easy way about him that drew her in.

Anna wandered into the bathroom and took a long shower that felt good after the long day yesterday. She dressed in jeans and a three-quarter sleeved blouse as well as cute but comfortable and sturdy leather shoes.

When she left her room, she found Josie and Pablo watching cartoons in the living room and she smiled and told them good morning. Tito and Maria were both at work. The only days her aunt and uncle took off were Sundays when they had their family rituals. First they would go to Sacred Heart Catholic Church where Anna sang in the choir. Afterward they always enjoyed a big Sunday lunch that Anna helped Maria cook.

Often on Sundays they would rent a movie and watch it in the evening while eating stove-popped popcorn and homemade candies like the ones Aunt Maria used to make when she and Tito had lived in Mexico. Sometimes they would have Mexican coconut sweets called *cocadas*, candied walnuts called *nueces garapiñadas*, or a milk fudge-like candy called *jamoncillo de leche.* She also made other Mexican desserts like *tres leches* cake and different varieties of flan. Aunt Maria had a sweet tooth, with a waistline that showed it, and the rest of the family happily ate whatever she made that Sunday.

After checking on the kids, Anna ate a light breakfast of one scrambled egg with a slice of toast and a small glass of orange juice. It wasn't that long until noon and she wasn't sure if she and Mike would be eating somewhere for lunch.

Carmen, the babysitter, showed up at eleven forty-five and immediately engaged the kids, who loved her. Carmen was in her mid-sixties and had retired from cleaning houses to babysit and she had a full schedule.

Two minutes before noon the doorbell rang. Josie shouted, "I'll get it," and Anna heard the five-year-old girl's shoes against the tile floor as she ran to the door.

With a frown, Anna worried her lower her lip. She wasn't sure if she should have let Josie answer the door, but there was no changing the fact that she was doing just that.

Anna squared her shoulders, straightened her spine, and walked into the living room, a smile coming easily to her lips when she saw Mike crouching in front of Josie, at her eye-level, listening to her. He glanced at Anna and his smile and penetrating gaze warmed her before he turned back to Josie who was chatting animatedly.

Mike's presence filled the room, making the large space seem small. She watched him talk to Josie and she drank in the sight, the comfort and ease Mike had in speaking with the little girl. He looked so good in his Stetson, a long-sleeved blue western shirt, dark blue Wrangler jeans, and broken-in brown boots.

Anna took in his tanned skin, his carved features, and the crinkles at the corners of his eyes when he smiled. His eyes, the color of polished oak, had an amused glint in them as he spoke with her young cousin.

"Josie." Anna found herself smiling, too. "I think you might be talking off Sheriff McBride's ears."

The girl giggled and Pablo walked up to them. Mike stood and extended his hand to eight-year-old Pablo who accepted it with a solemn look on his features. Mike introduced himself and Pablo told Mike his name. It was hard to believe Pablo was already eight—he'd grown so much in the past year. He was so serious lately, as if he needed to be a man of the house. Anna wondered if it was because his parents worked so much that they were rarely home.

"Pablo, Josie," Anna said as Mike and Pablo released hands. "Listen to Carmen. Only two hours of TV and one hour playing video games."

Pablo looked reluctant but said, "Yeah. Sure."

Josie smiled at Mike again before looking at Anna. "Okay, Anna," Josie said. She had an innocent expression backed with mischief that told Anna that her instructions were going in one ear and out the other.

Anna hugged Josie and squeezed Pablo's shoulder before she moved closer to Mike. She caught his scent, so spicy and masculine.

"Grab a jacket," he said. "It'll be cool this evening."

She nodded and took her jacket out of the closet before picking up her small purse from the table beside the front door. "Hold on a sec." She smiled at him and hurried to his room, returned with his blazer, and handed it to him. "Thank you for loaning it to me."

He took it from her. "Anytime."

Anna gave the kids and Carmen a smile. "I'll have my cell phone on if you need me." She gave them a wave goodbye before she and Mike stepped out of the doorway and Mike closed the door behind them.

"Your cousins look like great kids," Mike said as they walked down the front porch steps together.

"They are." She glanced up at Mike and wondered how he'd react to the truth about the children's parents.

Her thoughts darkened as she looked away. What had she gotten herself into?

It wasn't her doing. It was that bastard, Chad.

But for how long could she keep her secret? How long would she live afraid like she did, every single day?

As long as she had to. All she could do was pray.

"Everything okay?" Mike asked and she realized her face probably betrayed her emotions and concerns. She was too damned transparent sometimes.

"Great." She smiled up at him. "It's a gorgeous day." And it was, the fall air crisp and cool, along with a crystal clear, cloudless blue sky and a light breeze.

He returned her smile as they approached a black SUV that was pulled up to her curb. She recognized it as the vehicle she'd parked behind the night she'd met up with Mike at the bar. He opened the passenger door for her and helped her step up onto the running board and then she slid inside before he closed the door behind her. She set her jacket and purse beside her as he strode around to the driver's side and climbed in.

With a sexy little grin that turned her bones to water, he said, "Are you ready for a whopper of a day?"

His grin was so damned hot. "Most definitely," she said.

"Good." He laid the blazer on the back seat then started the SUV and put it into gear. "Ever been to a pumpkin festival before?"

"Is that where we're going?" She looked at him and felt another stir of excitement. "I've wanted to since we moved here. Something always seems to come up that keeps me from going."

He steered the vehicle down the neighborhood street. "I've been more times than I can count from the time I was a kid, but as far as I'm concerned, it never gets old."

During the eighteen-mile drive to the pumpkin farm in Dewey, Mike and Anna chatted. Mike had an easy way about him, comfortable and down-to-earth. She'd always been adept at talking with people, including strangers, so between the two of them there were no lulls in the conversation.

The drive was pleasant, the scenery beautiful. The local scenery never failed to amaze Anna. It was so pretty here, so filled with life. Her Aunt Maria would say she saw God in every living thing.

Cheerful looking signs and banners were erected at the entrance to the dirt road leading to the farm, a couple of flags fluttering in the breeze. Mike guided the SUV over a cattle guard and down a well-maintained dirt road toward a sprawling farmhouse with extensive barns and other buildings.

Mike drove the SUV into an area that had been reserved for parking. Once he'd shut off the engine and climbed out, he came around the vehicle and opened the door for Anna. He took her hand in his warm one and helped her out of the SUV.

He released her hand once she was out of the vehicle and she missed his touch at once. She looked at him and he smiled. The way his smile did queer things to her belly made her realize she was in trouble.

Big trouble.

CHAPTER 6

The positive vibes and laughter in the air as Mike and Anna walked up to the festival entrance made her feel almost giddy, as if she was a young girl at a carnival for the first time. On top of a hay bale, a tall sign listed entry fees and prices for trail rides, pony rides, and a haunted house. Mike paid the entry fees and they walked through the gateway lined with hay bales and pumpkins.

After they entered, they stopped and looked at another sign, this one giving times for festival singers and jugglers during the day and fireworks and a barn dance at night. Pumpkins of all sizes were everywhere. Tractors with long beds filled with hay bales for hayrides were parked near the bounce house.

A bounce house for kids was near the huge barn and a sign declaring "Corn Maze" was positioned in an opening that led into a field of tall corn. Another field was filled with pumpkins and there was also an apple orchard. According to a sign, they were each allowed to pick out a pumpkin from the field, and select apples from the orchard.

"My aunt would love to make apple *empanadas*." Anna looked at Mike. "Do you like to cook?"

He gave her a crooked grin. "I can't say it's my favorite thing. I do like to eat, though. How about you?"

"I love to cook." She tucked long strands of hair behind her ear. "I think I got my love for it from my aunt."

Vendors selling kettle corn, candied apples, fudge, funnel cake, hotdogs, nachos, and other foods lined the walkway. The smells reminded Anna of going to a carnival, only here the scents were mixed with fresh country air.

Further down were game booths where players could attempt to knock down milk bottles, throw darts at a dartboard, and shoot rubber ducks bobbing in water. Stuffed animals of all sizes hung from hooks at the booths.

More vendors' stalls were after the game booths, these selling items like sunglasses, tie-dye T-shirts, and handmade jewelry.

Everywhere people greeted Mike with hellos and handshakes. He was friendly and personable, and still managed to guide Anna onward without spending too much time with the people greeting him. It was clear he was here to be with her.

On occasion his cell phone would vibrate and he would check the display to make sure an urgent message hadn't been sent. As sheriff he was never fully off-duty. He did it as unobtrusively as possible but Anna didn't mind. She knew it was part of his job, something he'd signed up for when he'd run for the position.

"Are you hungry?" Mike nodded to the hotdog vendor. "Looks like they have some top-notch gourmet food."

Anna laughed. "I would love something to eat."

They ordered hotdogs—two for Mike and one for Anna—along with sodas. "Have to save room for one of those candy apples and fudge," she said when he asked her if she wanted anything else to eat.

"Good thinking," he said as he paid for their lunch.

They found seats in time for the next performance and laughed as a juggler engaged the audience and started tossing balls and rings into the air that he handled easily. He ended the performance by juggling lit torches.

Anna and Mike finished eating and waited until the performance was over before leaving to explore more of the festival. Mike was still greeted frequently and they ran into several of his cousins. Anna had never seen so many good-looking males in one family as she had with the McBrides. Ryan was one of Mike's cousins that they stopped to chat with. Ryan was with his wife, Megan, along with their adorable three-year-old identical twin sons and two-year-old daughter.

Anna watched Mike crouch to interact with the three children. He had the kids grinning and chatting with him in no time.

"You're good with children," Anna said after they parted ways with the family.

"I like kids," Mike said. "My stepbrother, Garrett, and his wife, Ricki, just announced they're expecting a baby in the spring. Our parents are thrilled to have a grandbaby on the way." Mike smiled. "They want to know why the rest of us haven't gotten busy having kids."

"Do you want children?" Anna asked.

Mike gave her a long look. "Yes."

"Boys or girls?" she asked.

"Both." He grinned. "I've never been too sure about a girl, since I'd have to keep a shotgun around once she's old enough to date. But seeing Ryan's daughter…I'd have to say I wouldn't mind having a girl one bit."

"Same here." She thought about her cousins. "I've helped raise Josie and Pablo since they were born, and there's joy in raising both girls and boys."

They wandered on past the bounce house and stopped by the entrance to the corn maze. They looked toward the horse corral.

"I've never been on a horse." Anna tilted her head to the side as she looked at a small group that was saddled up and heading out for a trail ride. "They're gorgeous animals, but they're so big that I have to admit I'm a little afraid of them."

"I'll take you on a ride at my place some time if you like." He rested his hand on her shoulder and she felt the warmth of his hand through her blouse. "I have a mare that's gentle and perfect to learn on. You'll fall in love with Maggie."

Anna smiled. "I'd like that very much." Horses might make her a little nervous, but she trusted Mike and his assurances made her feel a little more relaxed about the thought of riding one of the huge animals.

"Want to try the corn maze or get your pumpkin and apples?" he asked.

"Pumpkin and apples first," she said. "I've got to get my courage up for the corn maze. I got lost in one once as a kid, so I tend to panic a little when it comes to things like that."

They went out to the pumpkin patch and selected one each. Anna's pumpkin was round and fat while Mike's was tall and not so fat. He carried them out to the SUV and when he came back they each picked a dozen juicy red apples.

After he took the apples to the vehicle and then returned, they went to the candy apple vendor. Mike picked out a traditional caramel-dipped apple while Anna went with one dipped in dark chocolate caramel with a dark chocolate coating.

"Yes," she said before he asked, "I adore chocolate. One can never have enough, and the darker the better." She smiled inwardly as she thought about how many times she thought of his eyes as chocolate brown. Yes, she loved chocolate.

He linked his fingers with hers as they started walking down the aisle past the vendors. With a grin, he said, "That's good to know."

She liked the feel of his hand around hers and her tummy did all kinds of flips and flops. The caramel apple was delicious—the apple was juicy and the chocolate absolutely yummy. She felt light of heart and found herself enjoying every moment of the day.

"Best date ever," she said. She finished off her caramel apple and tossed the stick into a garbage can. "Thank you for bringing me."

"I'm glad you came." He nodded toward the games. "Up to a little friendly competition?"

She nodded. "You bet."

They spent the next half hour playing games. She did well with knocking down the milk bottles but couldn't beat Mike at darts or shooting rubber ducks in the bin of water. By the time they were finished playing, Mike had won a large stuffed animal and he let her pick out one. She chose a stuffed alligator and he carried it while they continued enjoying the pumpkin festival.

As the day grew later, Mike left Anna to take the alligator to the SUV and to grab their jackets. While he was gone, she went to a glass-blowing booth and watched a man make a hand blown ornament.

Mike came up beside her when he returned. "Pretty amazing, isn't it?"

She nodded. "It's been fun watching the artist."

Mike continued to hold their jackets as they continued on.

When they reached a bobbing for apples booth, he gestured to the large tub and the floating apples. "Up for a little wager?"

"And what that might be?" she asked.

"If I get an apple, I get a kiss," he said with a sexy grin.

A thrill went through her as she took the jackets from him. "You'd better get that apple, Sheriff."

CHAPTER 7

The memory of how Mike had kissed her the night she'd met him at Nectars caused flutters in Anna's belly. She found herself holding her breath as he held his hands behind his back and leaned forward. Apples bobbed in the water and she wondered if he'd be able to get one.

He looked at her and winked, and she thought she'd swoon like a historical romance book heroine. He lowered his face to the water and she bit her lower lip as she watched him. She didn't have long to wait. His teeth sank into one of the red apples and he rose, holding the apple with his teeth.

She swallowed as he took the apple out of his mouth and with a grin, caught her by the waist and drew her close to him. His face was cool and wet against hers, but his mouth was warm and inviting as he kissed her, long and so very sweet.

When he drew away, applause burst around them. Anna blinked, trying to catch her breath as she looked to see a small crowd around them. Heat crept through her and she glanced at Mike to see him smiling. He dried his face off with a paper towel that was handed to him then tossed it. They shared the apple before he took the jackets from her. He grabbed her hand and they walked toward the corn maze.

Lips still tingling from Mike's kiss, she looked up at him. "What if we get lost?"

He grinned at her. "I can think of worse things than getting lost with you."

She loved the zings that shot through her belly when he smiled like that at her. "You lead the way."

When they entered the maze, he gripped her hand tighter. The corn towered over them, and she would have felt lost immediately if it hadn't been for his hold on her hand. Corn stalks swayed and leaves brushed her skin and the cool air smelled of earth and cornhusks.

As they walked through the maze, feeling more and more lost, they laughed and soon she was breathless from the laughter.

"I think we're going in circles," Mike said when they reached another junction. "What do you think? Right or left?"

She looked from left to right. It was already shaded in the cornfield but it seemed that the sun must be going down because the light was getting dimmer.

"Left." She nodded in that direction.

"Left it is." He smiled at her and led her behind him.

Moments later they finally made it out of the corn. He gave her a quick grin "I think that calls for another kiss."

He met her mouth with his and she held back a soft moan that would have slipped from her. The day had been amazing and she couldn't imagine how it could get any better than this.

When he raised his head she looked into his eyes. He had a way of making her feel special…wanted…needed.

The reason she was really with him hit her full force.

It wasn't too hard to pretend that she was with Mike because she liked him, because she truly did. But the reason she was there now—it made her stomach twist into a knot. What was she doing?

Her mind turned to the ones she loved. She had to do it. She had no choice.

Damn. She had to get herself together. She had to do this. *Damn Chad!*

She needed to be her positive self and set all other thoughts aside. Somehow she would spend time with Mike without breaking either one of their hearts. She could do that, right?

She was going about it the wrong way if that was her plan.

He took both of her hands and gave her a long searching look. "Is something wrong, Anna?"

The seesaw of feelings made it hard to smile, but she managed it. "Nope. I'm having a fantastic time."

He gave a slow nod and squeezed both her hands. "We're not done yet."

She made the decision to enjoy herself for the rest of the day. "I'm ready."

He released one of her hands and led her away from the cornfield toward a tractor and a flatbed trailer where people were climbing onto the bed and sitting on hay bales. Mike helped her up and climbed onto the flatbed. They found a hay bale to share and he brought her close to him so that his arm was around her shoulders and her body touched his from her shoulder to her knee.

She closed her eyes, pretending for a moment that this could be real. She knew she would have to back off, but for now she could pretend, couldn't she?

The tractor started moving, jostling them back and forth as the hayride took them through the apple orchard, around the barns and other buildings, as well as pens where cows grazed and horses swished their tails as they ate grain in their feeders.

As the hayride continued, the sky grew dark, the air chillier, and she shivered.

"Here." He held her jacket up and helped her slide her arms into it. He put on his own jacket and then held her closer.

It was dark as they came close to approaching the point where the hayride had started. Fireworks exploded overhead, causing Anna to catch her breath in surprise. The fireworks glittered in the night sky, raining down in red, orange, green, and blue sparkles. Everyone on the hayride oohed and ahhed.

The tractor stopped and they watched the show. She had never experienced anything so romantic as sitting beside Mike on a hayride near a pumpkin patch and a cornfield on a cool early October night. It was easy to pretend they were alone as they sat close, her head on his shoulder.

When the fireworks display ended, she looked at Mike and she smiled. He lowered his head and kissed her as the hayride started again.

He moved his hand to her face and brushed her cheek with his knuckles. "There's no one I would have rather shared today with than you, Anna."

She didn't know what to say so she kissed him.

The tractor came to a halt and she drew away. It was easy to forget she was being blackmailed as she spent time with Mike. It was so comfortable being with him.

After everyone else who had been on the hayride climbed off, Mike jumped from the flatbed then helped Anna down. When she was on the ground, she brushed hay from the seat of her pants with both hands.

He took her hand again. "Know how to dance to country music?" he asked.

She shook her head. "I never learned how."

"I'll bet you're a quick learner," he said.

"I'm willing to give it a shot sometime," she said.

"You're in luck." He put his arm around her shoulders. "A barn dance is supposed to start after the fireworks."

Anna couldn't believe how happy it made her to know that the evening wasn't over yet. "Well, let's go, then."

They wandered toward the barn that was lit up, a live band playing, music pouring through the open double doors.

Anna caught the delicious smell of barbeque just as Mike said, "Damn, that smells good. Hungry?"

She nodded. "Most definitely."

"Why don't you reserve us a place to sit and I'll be right back," he said.

While she waited for him, she sat at a picnic table and looked around. Couples crowded the area, laughing and chatting. She felt a part of something like she'd never felt before. She wondered at that. Maybe it was because she didn't have much of a life beyond family and work. It was good to get out and have a good time with someone she wanted to spend time with.

When Mike returned, he set a plate of pulled pork in front of her before sitting next to her on the bench and placing his own plate on the table. The plate was filled not only with BBQ meat but cornbread, pinto beans, and coleslaw.

From his jacket pockets he produced napkins, plastic utensils, and two cans of Coke. He popped the tab on one Coke and set it in front of her before opening his own.

The BBQ was delicious and she loved the buttered cornbread. She watched people around them in between eating and talking with Mike.

Like it had been throughout the day, people would stop and tell Mike hello and good luck with the election. He was always friendly with a genuine smile. A couple of times people had attempted to get started on a political topic, but Mike had gracefully managed to get out of the conversation.

"So do you kiss babies, too?" she asked in a teasing tone after Mike shook a man's hand before the man continued on with a woman toward the barn.

Mike grinned. "Only beautiful women named Anna."

Her whole body tingled. "Is that right?"

He gave a solemn nod before giving her a quick kiss. "Absolutely," he said when he drew away.

When they finished eating their meal, Mike took their plates, napkins, plastic utensils, and Coke cans to a garbage can. He brought back a plate of goodies for them to share from a table filled with cakes, cookies, brownies, pies, apple bars, and other treats. By the time Anna had eaten a piece of apple pie, she was stuffed.

She held up her hand when he offered her a brownie. "Nooo. I'm so full," she said with a shake of her head.

After Mike had tossed the dessert plate, he placed his fingers at the base of her spine and guided her into the barn. The band was good, the music loud. It wasn't long until Mike had her on the dance floor, teaching her how to two-step and country waltz as well as swing dance. She and Mike chose not to participate in a couple of line dances but she enjoyed watching them.

It wasn't long before she was breathless from laughing and dancing, and a light sheen of perspiration was on her skin. Just as she was going to beg off another dance, a slow song started.

He swept her into his arms and held her close as they moved around the dance floor. He was so much taller than her that she had to tilt her head to look up at him. Their eyes met and held, and he lowered his face to hers and gave her a soft kiss that made her even more breathless than she already was.

She was so close to him that she felt his phone vibrate against her and she drew away from the kiss.

"I wish I could ignore that," he said with a frown.

"I understand." She gave him a smile. "Go ahead."

He pulled the phone out of the holster on his belt, checked the screen, then read a text message. "Damn," he said. He looked at her. "I've got to get to a scene. I'll drop you off on my way." He squeezed her shoulders. "I'm sorry, sweetheart."

"Don't be." She gave him a smile and added, "Let's go."

CHAPTER 8

The day had been amazing. Anna smiled as she sat in her seat in the SUV after Mike had helped her into the vehicle. She waited for him to go around it to the driver's side. When he opened the door, she saw that he was taking his cell phone out of its holster. When he climbed in, he was already talking.

"Hey, John." Mike started the SUV. "Just got notified that a group of ten to fifteen undocumented aliens have been located, along with over a hundred pounds of marijuana."

Anna's skin went cold as Mike continued, "On my way to the scene after I make a quick stop. Called to let you know that one of the illegals mentioned Jesus Perez." Mike listened before he said, "I'll keep you posted."

Feeling stiff and frozen, Anna didn't move, but her heart thundered against her breastbone.

Mike signed off with John before sliding the phone back into the belt holster. He put the SUV in reverse and gave Anna an apologetic look before looking in his mirrors and backing up the vehicle. "Not exactly the way I wanted to end the night," he said.

She forced a smile. "It was a wonderful day."

He glanced at her and smiled. "It was."

The trip back was quieter than the drive from Prescott had been. Mike seemed lost in thought and Anna felt sick in her belly. The reason they were returning to Prescott hit too close to home.

When they reached her home and parked, he once again went to her side of the vehicle and helped her out of the SUV. After they gathered the alligator, her pumpkin, and a crate of apples, he walked her up the stairs to her door. She opened it and saw that no one was in the living room. She told him to set the apples and pumpkin just inside the door on the floor and she put down the alligator. She'd take care of it all later.

They stepped back onto the porch and he cupped her face in his hands and gave her a soft kiss. "Let's continue where we left off later. I'll call you Monday morning."

She nodded. "Talk with you then."

He gave her a quick kiss then waited for her to go into her house. She paused. "Thank you again for today," she said.

"My pleasure." He touched the brim of his hat and turned away to jog down the steps.

She closed the door and locked it behind her. Chilled through to the bone, she rested her forehead against the door and closed her eyes. What was she doing? It could have been her aunt and uncle who'd been discovered.

Was there any way to get out from under the dark cloud of Chad's blackmail? It wasn't right. How could he do this to her and her family?

Easy. He was a bastard who cared for nothing but himself and obviously had no scruples when it came to an ethical way to run a campaign.

A deep shuddering breath went through her and she picked up the alligator and hugged it tight. She had to talk to Chad, had to make him see that this was a bad idea.

Not only because of the danger to her family, but the danger to her heart and Mike's as well.

* * * * *

Mike's thoughts slid from the scene he was approaching to Anna. It had been clear she was enjoying herself but hadn't minded when they had to leave early. But something had changed. It had been barely noticeable, but he was naturally perceptive as well as being trained to notice emotional changes. Anna's emotions had definitely shifted.

When he arrived at the scene, red and blue lights flashed from sheriff's department and Customs and Border Patrol vehicles. A group of men and women sat on the ground against a fence in front of a house with cracked and peeling white paint and a porch that barely looked safe enough to step on. Lights blazed from within the house as sheriff's department deputies and U.S. Border Patrol agents went in and out through the front door.

Mike parked his SUV and climbed out. He approached Sam Davies, a senior agent with the Border Patrol.

When Mike reached Davies, the agent greeted him with a nod. "Sheriff."

Mike returned the greeting and gestured to the undocumented aliens, UDAs. "How many?"

"Twelve UDAs total. Eight men and four women," Davies said. "We also seized about 70 kilos of marijuana."

Mike watched the agents carrying out bundles. One hundred and fifty pounds was a good haul of marijuana. "I understand a tip came in."

"Anonymous. Could have been a neighbor or someone associated with the coyotes who are smuggling in the UDAs, for all we know." Davies nodded toward the men and women sitting on the ground along the fence. "From what we've gathered the coyotes have barely been giving them any food. They're weak from hunger."

"Any of the coyotes here when you raided the place?" Mike asked.

Davies shook his head. "All we found here were the UDAs and the marijuana."

Mike blew out his breath. "Damn."

A vehicle came to a hard stop, skidding in the gravel in front of the house. Davies and Mike looked to see a reporter and cameraman climbing out of a van with Channel 7 News on the side.

"Who the hell called the press?" Davies muttered.

Mike shook his head. How reporters managed to end up wherever Mike went was a mystery. Sometimes he wondered if there was a leak in his department. The news could put a negative or positive spin on the bust. One, the success in tracking down illegal aliens and an illegal substance. Or two, how human and drug trafficking was only getting worse, which this bust helped to prove.

The reporter, Paige Windhaven, approached Davies and Mike while the cameraman filmed the scene.

"Sheriff," Paige said, microphone in hand. "What can you tell us about tonight's bust?"

"I'm out of here," Davies muttered so that only Mike could hear.

"Thanks," Mike said dryly.

Fact was, as sheriff it was Mike's job to be in the spotlight and handle reporters. Whether or not he pulled off a good interview with reporters depended on the situation.

He spoke several minutes with the reporter, giving her what he knew about this bust. He also gave a comment that gave his stance on human trafficking, something that was expected of him. It was his job to uphold the laws, and that was exactly what the sheriff's department and the Border Patrol were doing.

As soon as he could, he excused himself and headed off to join his deputies. He mentally shook his head. His least favorite part of the job was the publicity, but it came with the territory.

When he reached his deputies, he spoke to Sergeant Reg Schmidt. "What have you found out about the connection to Jesus Perez?"

Schmidt was a harsh man and spoke in a hard tone. He gave a nod toward one of the UDAs sitting against the fence. "According to Luis there, the name Perez has been tossed around. Luis thinks Perez is the head honcho, but isn't sure the bastard has actually ever been here."

"Well, hell." Mike looked at the house. "Any other names come up?"

"Yeah." Schmidt nodded. "But none I've ever heard of before." Schmidt gave him the names.

"Can't say I'm familiar with them." Mike rocked back on his boot heels. "Must be new to the area."

"New delivery service," Schmidt said.

Mike stayed at the scene until the last of the deputies and BP agents were leaving. The reporter and photographer had hung around for a while but eventually left.

When he was finally on his way home, he allowed his thoughts to turn back to Anna as he drove. It had been a hell of a good day—up until he'd had to go to the bust.

His gut told him that Anna Batista was a hell of a woman, and might just be the one he'd been waiting for. His gut was usually right on, and he was confident he was right about Anna.

She was so damned beautiful. She'd had a good sense of humor when he'd teased her, was intelligent, fun, and he enjoyed being around her. He'd never felt like this around any other woman.

It had been some time since he'd been in a relationship. Being a public figure and doing his job as sheriff hadn't left a lot of time for a relationship or much of a private life. Everything he did was scrutinized.

He frowned as he thought about that. It was too soon to start thinking of long-term with Anna, but he still wondered how she would handle being in a relationship with a man in the spotlight, not to mention the fact he was a lawman.

With a shake of his head he pushed his thoughts away from the permanent and focused on the here and now. He'd take it one day at a time with Anna.

CHAPTER 9

In Sacred Heart Catholic Church, Anna stood with the choir, waiting as the priest conducted mass. She clenched her hymnal, tried to push distracting thoughts out of her mind, and concentrate on the mass.

It did no good. Her thoughts bounced from the amazing time she'd had yesterday at the pumpkin festival with Mike, to the moment he had to leave and the reason why, to Chad's blackmail. She knew she should go to confession, but she was afraid of what the priest would say. What might he consider to be the right thing to do? What if he thought she should have her aunt and uncle turn themselves in?

A sick feeling bottomed out her stomach. What would she do if they were deported?

What about Josie and Pablo?

Jaci elbowed Anna in the side and she jumped. Everyone in the choir had raised their hymnal and Sister Gracie was standing in front of them, ready to lead them in a hymn. Anna raised her own hymnal and waited for the cue from the nun.

Anna was grateful for the reprieve from her thoughts. Her voice rose with the choir as they sang *If Ye Love Me*. She focused on singing each verse with her heart and soul.

As she sang, she glanced at the place where her family was sitting—and faltered in song. Chad Johnson was sitting beside her cousin, Josie.

Anna's throat seemed to close off as Chad gave her a knowing look. He glanced at her family and then back to Anna and smiled.

Flames burned her cheeks as she forced herself to continue singing. She couldn't look away from Chad as he smirked at her. Finally, she was able to tear her gaze from his and back to Sister Gracie's as the last strains of the hymn faded. The sister turned to face Father Bernard, who then continued to conduct mass.

Every word that was spoken was nothing but a buzz in Anna's ears as she was hyperaware of Chad sitting next to her family. Chad was not Catholic and she had never seen him at mass. She knew that he attended the Baptist church with Chandra. His presence here was a message to her—he knew about her family and was making sure she knew he was serious in his blackmail.

The rest of the service passed in a blur. Even after accepting the sacrament, she was on autopilot. She went through the ritual of shaking hands with those around her and giving the traditional greeting, "Peace be with you," and receiving the response back, "And also with you." She barely head the words.

As Father Bernard walked down the center aisle at the end of the service, she and the rest of the choir sang a final hymn, *Nunc*

Dimittis. The parishioners followed the priest outside the church. There was much greeting, talking, and smiling as usual.

Anna was praying that Chad wouldn't be there when she walked out of the church. But when she made it out into the sunlight, Chad stood to the side on the church steps, talking with Uncle Tito and her Aunt Maria with Josie and Pablo standing nearby.

Heart pounding, she walked up to Chad and her aunt and uncle. She tried to sound normal as she said, "Hi, Chad." She smiled at her aunt and uncle. "I assume you've met Chandra's brother, Chad?"

Her aunt and uncle nodded and smiled at Chad. "It is nice to meet your friends, *hija*," Uncle Tito said. Even though he was her uncle, he still called Anna daughter in Spanish because she was like one to him and her aunt.

"Are you staying for refreshments?" Aunt Maria asked Chad. "I brought my *tres leches* cake, Anna's favorite."

Anna held her breath, hoping Chad would say no.

Chad looked at Anna and smiled. "I would love to."

Anna swallowed. "Why don't we go before all of the cake is gone?"

Uncle Tito chuckled. "Maria's cakes are popular."

Maria gave an approving smile, as if she thought Chad was there because he was interested in her in a romantic way.

Trying to look relaxed, Anna hooked her arm in her aunt's with Josie taking her opposite hand. Tears pushed at the backs of Anna's eyes and she struggled to keep a single tear from falling. This was her family, the people she loved, and Chad was threatening them to blackmail her.

Refreshments were always in a large basement room at the back of the church. Anna wasn't hungry but took a piece of her aunt's cake and ate it so that her aunt wouldn't worry that she was ill. Heaven forbid that Anna imply she wasn't feeling well. Aunt Maria would be mothering her the rest of the day.

When Aunt Maria and Uncle Tito were occupied, talking with friends, Anna turned to find Chad standing behind her. He was holding a paper cup filled with punch and he took a drink while his eyes met hers.

"What are you doing here?" she demanded in a low tone.

He lowered his cup. "Just making sure you're doing what I asked you to." He gave such a fake smile that she wanted to slap him.

"I'm doing what you are *blackmailing* me to do." She clenched one hand into a fist, the other holding the plate with what was left of her cake. "Stay away from my family."

"Blackmail?" He raised his brows. "All I did was ask you to get in good with Sheriff McBride."

"That's a load of—" She took a deep breath and let it out. "Call it whatever you want, but you know it is blackmail."

"As long as you know I'm serious, we're fine." Chad gave a shrug of one shoulder. "Make sure you update me regularly." He drank from his punch cup.

She really, really wanted to slap him. Instead she gritted her teeth then said, "I went out with him yesterday. I'll start working on his campaign on Monday."

"I'm impressed." Chad smiled and nodded. "You're working faster than I expected. Look what can be accomplished when you're properly motivated."

She thought seriously about smashing the rest of her cake into his face but managed to restrain herself. "I'll be in touch if I learn anything that might be of use to you." She said the last words with distaste.

"Good." Chad tossed his empty paper cup into a nearby garbage can. "I'll plan on talking with you soon."

Anna clenched her jaw as she watched him wend his way through the crowded room.

"Is something wrong, *hija*?" Aunt Maria laid her hand on Anna's arm.

Anna fixed a smile on her face and faced her aunt. "Not at all. I'm just a little tired. I had a long day and evening yesterday."

"You should rest when we get home," Maria said.

With a shake of her head, Anna put her hand over her aunt's. "I'm fine. I'm going to help with Sunday dinner as usual."

Maria raised her other hand and patted Anna's. "Are you ready to go home?"

"Yes." Anna felt some relief as her aunt let her concern slide. "Is everyone else set to go?"

Maria nodded toward the door. "Tito is waiting with *mis hijos* outside," she said, referring to Uncle Tito and her children. Even though Maria preferred to speak English, she would slip into Spanish at times.

Once they were in Anna's Honda and left the church, they reached home in no time. For dinner, Maria and Anna made homemade flour tortillas along with *carnitas,* a tender and juicy fried pork; *arroz con frijoles negro*, which was black beans and rice; and *pico de gallo*, a traditional salsa. It was a simple dinner, but Uncle Tito's favorite.

As they ate dinner, Anna looked around at the people she loved and wondered if they should move. With Chad knowing the truth and the chance that he might report her aunt and uncle, maybe she should convince them that they should pick up and go. No matter how much they enjoyed their lives in Prescott, they could always start over somewhere else. They'd done it before, when they left Bisbee.

There were no easy answers. She could do as Chad had blackmailed her to do, and still be discovered.

Anna let her breath out slowly, trying to release the tension in her body. She smiled and nodded to her aunt and uncle as they spoke about work, and she listened as Pablo talked about his activities in third grade. Josie had just turned five and would start kindergarten in the fall.

Deciding to enjoy her family, Anna pushed thoughts aside of Chad, Mike, and everything else that tore at her heart. She needed to take this all one day at a time—it was all she could do at this moment. Maybe they'd have to move, maybe not. But for now she needed to be present for the ones she loved.

She spent the rest of the day teasing her young cousins and laughing with them as well as her aunt and uncle. She let the day unfold as every Sunday did, allowing herself to enjoy the time she had with her family.

A family she loved with every part of her heart and soul.

* * * * *

Mike slapped his Stetson against his thigh, shaking off the dust as he walked toward his cousin Jayson's truck. He'd had just driven onto Mike's property, hauling a horse trailer behind his vehicle.

The afternoon sun shone brightly in the clear, cloudless sky and the still air was cool against his face. A horse's whinny came from the direction of the corral.

Dust rose from around the tires as Jayson parked his truck. He killed the engine, opened his door, and jumped out. "How's it going, Sheriff?" Jayson asked with a grin as he rounded the vehicle.

"Just fine." Mike met up with Jayson and slapped him on his shoulder. "Any cattle get out while your fence was down the other night?"

Jayson nodded. "Took us a good part of the night to round up about twenty head and get them back on my property. Repairing the fence was the easy part. Helped that the moon was bright."

They walked toward the back of the trailer where the backside of a horse was visible. Jayson unlocked the back gate and swung it open. He patted the horse's rump. "Let's go, little girl."

It didn't take much coaxing before the beautiful mare was out of the horse trailer. Jayson held the Quarter horse by her halter while Mike took a good look at her.

Mike stroked the sorrel's neck as he admired her. "She's a fine mare."

Jayson nodded his agreement. "Dancer is one of my favorites. Have to say I'm going to miss her. She's a little headstrong sometimes, but she's got a good disposition."

"You'll get visitation in a couple of months when it comes time to breed her," Mike said. "That stallion of yours is among the finest in the state."

"Firestarter sure is." Jayson stroked Dancer's muzzle. "Comes from a long line of champion stock."

Jayson gave a slight tug on the halter and he and Mike fell into step with the horse as they headed toward the barn. The mare's hooves made a clopping sound on the hard packed earth as they walked.

"A shame you had to put down that Appaloosa," Jayson said.

"She was a good mare." Mike reached for the latch to the barn door and pushed it open. He'd had Viv for twenty-two years before the accident with a delivery truck that broke both of her front legs and caused her to have internal bleeding. A sense of loss always accompanied thoughts of the mare. They'd been together a good long time.

Once they were in the barn, Mike put Dancer in a stall and removed her halter. He gave her a flake of alfalfa hay, and checked the watering trough before closing the stall door. His other two horses were out in the corral.

When they left Dancer alone in the stall, Jayson hooked his thumbs in his front pockets and walked out of the barn into the sunshine. "How's the campaign going?"

"Last I checked I was still up in the polls, but not by much." Mike raised his Stetson and pushed his fingers through his hair before settling the hat back on his head. "Chad is a tough opponent."

"Can't be easy going up against someone willing to cross lines like Chad." Jayson scowled. "I wouldn't put it past him if he got dirty on this one."

"If he does, let's hope the voters see through him." Mike shrugged. "I don't intend to stoop to his level."

Jayson pushed up the brim of his hat, a thoughtful look on his features. "Have you thought about what you'll do next if he wins the election? Get back on with the police force or maybe work in the private sector?"

"I've thought a lot about that question." Mike let his gaze drift over his scaled-back ranch and pictured it as a much larger operation. "I'm considering going into ranching full-time."

"You'd be damned good at it." Jayson slapped Mike on the shoulder. "You're a McBride. As Aunt Gert would say, 'It's in your blood. You can try and take a McBride out of the country, but there's no way to take the country out of a McBride.'"

"That's true." Mike rocked back on his heels and smiled as he thought of his spinster great-aunt, sister of his deceased grandfather. "How do you think Aunt Gert would feel about letting the press in for our annual McBride Halloween party?"

Jayson considered it for a moment. "I don't think she would mind. Gert is keen on you winning the election. The whole family is, for that matter. So I'd say yeah, bring 'em on in."

"I'll check with Gert to make sure she's fine with it," Mike said.

"I've got to get going." Jayson reached the driver's side of his truck. "If I don't catch you at the Halloween party, I'll see you at John and Hollie's wedding."

Mike gave a nod. "Not long from now."

As Jayson drove off, Mike headed for the barn. The breeze kicked up, bending dry grass and causing tree leaves to flutter. The smell of fall was in the air.

When he reached the barn, he went to Dancer's stall. "How're you doing, girl?" The horse came up to him and looked at him with her big, intelligent brown eyes. He stroked her muzzle. "You have some big shoes to fill. Viv was my sweetheart. But I think you'll do just fine here."

Dancer snuffled his hand where it rested on the stall door, her muzzle velvety against his skin. "Looking for a treat?" He stroked her neck. "I might have a little something for you as we get better acquainted."

After he retrieved the mare's halter and put it on her, he took her out of the stall. He took the lid off of a barrel filled with horse pellets and grabbed several. He pocketed a few then held out a couple of the giant pellets for her to take from his palm. Her breath was warm, her muzzle soft as she lipped the treats.

She stood patiently as he began brushing her down. He spoke to her in an even tone, letting her get used to his voice and his touch.

Mike's thoughts turned to Jayson's question regarding what he'd do if he lost the race to Chad. Mike crouched to brush the mare's foreleg. He'd given it a lot of thought and if he did lose the sheriff's race, he'd still want to be involved with the community and contribute to it in some way. It was something he needed to get his head around as to where he'd want to put his efforts.

He shifted and moved to Dancer's other foreleg and started brushing it. He'd get into ranching full time and maybe even start a family. An image of Anna came to mind and he found himself smiling. What was it about her that had him thinking of serious relationships and even expanding the McBride brood?

A family was something he knew he'd like to have someday. And right now he knew he was getting way ahead of himself…but just maybe someday would be here sooner than he'd thought.

CHAPTER 10

A queer feeling settled in Anna's belly as she walked toward Mike's campaign headquarters and she hugged her blazer closer. The chill she felt wasn't from the cold outside, it was from what was eating her on the inside. She might as well be called a spy or a mole, because that's what she was—a spy for Chad, a mole to help him find dirt on Mike.

The feeling clenching her insides threatened to make her ill as she reached the headquarters' door in an office building on Gurley Street. Mike would hate her if he found out she was spying on him. But if she did what Chad said, she could only pray that Mike would never know.

She pasted on a smile as she pulled open the door and walked into the room. Red, white, and blue professional campaign posters and signs greeted her that stated:

Mike McBride
Yavapai County
Sheriff

Simple and to the point. His last name was big and bold and Sheriff was large, italicized and written in blue and red. The "e" had a sheriff's star in it.

Anna looked around the empty reception area. She heard sounds and voices on the other side of the cubicle wall that separated the reception desk from the rest of the office. She smoothed down her blouse and slacks with her palms and wondered if she should wait here or go find someone. Hopefully that someone would be Mike.

A tall, pretty woman with short brunette hair walked around a corner. The woman, who must have been in her late fifties, greeted Anna with a smile on her lips and in her warm, hazel eyes.

The woman held out her hand. "I'm Angel McBride, Mike's stepmother."

"It's nice to meet you." Anna took Angel's hand. "I'm Anna Batista."

"I've been expecting you." Angel released Anna's hand. "Mike will be here anytime now. In the meantime, come on in and meet the others."

Anna walked at Mike's stepmother's side and met Hollie Simmons, soon to be John McBride's wife. Anna remembered seeing the former kindergarten teacher's picture in the newspaper and on news reports when she was wrongly jailed for the murder of her stepbrother. Hollie reminded Anna of a southern belle with her gentle manners and lovely personality.

Anna also greeted Megan, who she had met along with her husband and children, at the pumpkin festival. Megan was a natural with computers, websites, the Internet, as well as graphic design. A curvy brunette, she had glass-green eyes and a wide smile. For the few hours a day that she worked at the campaign office, she had a sitter stay with her children.

Moments later, Mike walked in, filling the room with his very presence. He had an easy, engaging, good-natured manner about him, but there was no mistaking he was a man who was serious when he needed to be and who took charge of any situation he might find himself in.

Anna looked at him and felt an immediate sense of elation followed by longing, and then the sick sense of the betrayal that was being forced on her.

She worked up a smile as he neared her. She must have done a fairly good job at it because he smiled in return.

"I've introduced Anna to Megan and Hollie," Angel said. "She's all yours now." Angel gave Anna a little wink before she left to return to work on the campaign.

"Why don't we talk over coffee about what you'll be doing for my campaign?" he asked. "We can walk on over to Sweet Things."

She loved the timbre of his voice and the way his warm brown eyes focused on her as he spoke. "I'd like that." She felt like her voice sounded small in comparison to the power in his tone. "During the time I've lived in Prescott, I've never gone to that bakery."

He smiled down at her. "You don't know what you've been missing."

With his fingers touching the small of her back, he escorted her out of the HQ. His simple touch sent frissons of desire through her. She swallowed, glad he couldn't sense her pulse quickening and the tingles running rampant throughout her body.

When they entered Sweet Things, a pretty blonde was arranging pastries in a glass display case. She rose as she saw Mike and Anna. Bells jangled at the top of the door as Mike closed it behind them.

The blonde smiled at them. "Hi, Mike."

Mike and Anna reached the glass case that Ricki stood behind. "How's it going, Ricki?" Mike asked. "How are you feeling?"

Ricki rested her hand on her belly and smiled. "Junior and me are doing great."

"Good." Mike grinned. "Little McBrides are popping up all over the place like daisies."

Ricki laughed. "They certainly are."

"I'd like to introduce you to Anna Batista." He turned to Anna. "Anna, this is Ricki, who owns Sweet Things. She is yet another cousin's wife."

"What a prolific family the McBrides are." It was Anna's turn to smile. "Great to meet you, Ricki, and congratulations."

Ricki positively glowed. "Thank you."

A thought flittered through Anna's mind. What would it be like to be pregnant with her own child? *With Mike's child?*

The thought sent instant heat to her cheeks and she hurried to find something to say.

"Your bakery smells wonderful." Anna's gaze drifted over cases filled with Napoleons, cream puffs, éclairs, petit fours, cookies, doughnuts, and so much more. "And everything looks amazing."

"Everything *is* amazing," Mike said. "I think I've tried just about everything at least once."

Anna glanced at Mike and then Ricki. "With everything looking so darn good, how am I supposed to choose?"

Mike wore an amused expression. "We can share a few things if you'd like and then you'll get to taste a variety."

"I could go for a little hot coffee." Anna noticed pots of coffee on a drink station behind Ricki. "I'll take one with room for cream."

Mike picked out several pastries, paid for them, and then they headed toward one of the small tables along the large plate glass window. The window had *Sweet Things* written in a curve across the glass with *Bakery* beneath that.

Through the glass Anna saw people walking along the sidewalks. Some were obviously tourists visiting this quaint part of town while others were clearly residents going about their busy day.

Prescott attracted tourists year round. The town was rich in history with its famous Whiskey Row and abundant historical landmarks, including the town's "Plaza" that had been honored as one of the "Top Ten Public Spaces" in the U.S. The town had more than 700 homes and businesses listed in the National Register of Historic Places along with galleries, antique stores, and other shops.

Anna slipped off her blazer and hung it on the back of the chair before sitting. Displaying his innate courtesy, Mike waited for her to sit before he took his own seat. With a plate of goodies between them, they began talking about the campaign.

"I'd like you to focus on three things," Mike said after swallowing a bite of a Napoleon. "Setting up some kind of hand-shaking appearance, arranging another debate, and coverage of the family Halloween party."

"That's great." Anna felt a burst of enthusiasm. "So your family won't mind letting reporters in on the family event?"

"I called Aunt Gert this morning and she was all for it." Mike gave a little grin. "She sounded downright excited at the prospect."

"That's terrific." Anna held half an éclair in one hand, trying not to let the cream slide out. "I can make the arrangements. It will be fun," she said before taking a bite of the éclair.

Mike cut a cannoli in half. "You're also invited to come as my guest."

Anna dabbed her lips with her napkin. "I'd love to."

"You missed a little." Mike reached across the table and brushed her cheek with his thumb and she went still. Her heart beat at a rapid pace as his gaze met and held hers. He slowly let his fingers slide away from her face, never breaking eye contact.

She swallowed as he lowered his hand to rest on the table. "Thank you." The words came out in a near whisper.

The corner of his mouth quirked into a smile just for her, making her feel warm all over. "Anytime."

The bells on the door jangled as customers came into the bakery, the sound and movement breaking the connection that had held them together in that long moment.

Mike began talking about the campaign and she let out her breath. Her feelings toward him were growing so intense that she felt like her emotions were careening out of control. She needed to take a step back. Put some distance between them and just work with him in a professional capacity. She would be close enough to him still to…

To spy on him.

Her stomach sank. This was wrong on so many levels.

My family, she reminded herself. *I've got to think about them.*

Mike paused and she realized he was studying her. "Is everything all right?" he asked.

She had to work at it but she did manage to smile. "Everything is great. I can't wait to get started."

"Good." Mike seemed genuinely pleased to have her on board, and as she laid out ideas he endorsed them whole-heartedly.

"You've got a talent for this." Mike settled back in his seat when they finished discussing the three events he wanted her to handle. "I think I've found a secret weapon." He said it in a way that was so genuine and heartfelt that it made her warm inside.

She had just taken the last bite of her half of the cannoli, chewed, and swallowed it. "That remains to be seen." She wiped her mouth and her fingers off with a paper napkin. "I still have to prove my worth."

He gave a low chuckle. "With your ideas and your event planning background, not to mention your professionalism, I have no doubt that you will be extraordinary."

She tried not to think any more about her duplicity. "I appreciate your confidence in me."

He studied her a long moment. He seemed to do that often and she found it both unnerving and somehow thrilling. Like he could see deep down into her soul and liked what he saw.

"It's not going to be easy to beat Chad Johnson." Mike gave a little smile. "He's a tough and worthy opponent."

No he's not, Anna thought with a viciousness that was so different from how she usually was. *He's not worthy enough to polish your shoes.*

She remembered what she'd been told, that there was bad blood between Mike and Chad. Mike was being more courteous than she imagined Chad would ever be. Should she ask what it was between them? She mentally shook her head. No, it wasn't any of her business.

Mike gathered the plate and coffee mugs, which he returned to Ricki while Anna tossed the paper napkins. Anna took her jacket off the back of her chair and Mike helped her slip it on.

"It was great meeting you," Anna said to Ricki, giving her a little wave as Mike opened the door.

"Come back and see me." Ricki said. "Mike needs to get in here more often."

He grinned and touched the brim of his Stetson as he gave her a little nod. "Take care of yourself, Ricki."

The bells at the top of the door jangled again as it closed behind them and they started back to the campaign HQ.

CHAPTER 11

Angel set Anna up at the one empty desk and caught her up on the campaign. Anna set to work on the events Mike wanted her to handle.

While she worked, she couldn't get her mind to stray far from Chad having shown up at church yesterday and his threat. A tight knot stayed in her chest that wouldn't go away.

What could she possibly tell Chad?

From Angel, Anna got the details about the Halloween party being hosted by Mike's great-aunt Gert, as well as Gert's address and phone number. Anna also called Gert and introduced herself, and asked if the elder woman had any questions or preferences since it was her home. The woman was enthusiastic about having coverage of the party for her nephew's campaign and she went on and on about how he was the best sheriff Yavapai County had ever known. Anna enjoyed talking with Gert. Afterward, Anna made the arrangements for press coverage.

It was close to two now, so she had plenty of time left to work on putting together a handshaking event or the final debate. She hadn't decided on the handshaking opportunity just yet. She needed to see if there were any special events going on in Prescott.

Her concentration drifted and she glanced out the window at the clear sky and rested her chin on her palm, her elbow on the desk. She watched cars passing by and people walking down the sidewalks. So many people going on with their lives. She bit the end of her pen as she got lost in her thoughts.

For a moment she thought about Chandra and how much she missed her friend. The lunches, the shopping, the laughing, and sharing. There was so much she would tell Chandra if circumstances were different. Anna hoped that one day the two of them could patch things up. The mess things were in, though… She didn't know if things could ever go back the way they were, even between her and her best friend.

Anna continued to immerse herself in the work at the office, not allowing herself to think about anything but helping Mike as much as she could. She enjoyed the challenge and she liked the fact that she was doing something that would aid his campaign. Maybe there would be nothing for her to give Chad and he'd give up.

But that was too easy. He wasn't going to give up.

With a sigh, she closed her eyes and wished things were different. Under other circumstances, Mike was someone she could have fallen in love with easily. But she couldn't, due to her family. And if he ever found out she'd been sent to spy on him, well, that would be the end of everything.

The nape of her neck tingled and she sensed a nearby presence. She opened her eyes, startled, and dropped the pen on the desk when she saw Mike sitting in one of the two chairs in front of her desk.

He looked delicious in his Stetson and sheriff's uniform as he reclined in the chair. Every line of his carved features, every cut of his muscles, every bit of him radiated an intense alpha-maleness that set her hormones on fire.

Even as he appeared relaxed in his seat, there was a feeling of motion that she couldn't explain. Like he was always thinking, always analyzing, always planning his next move and mentally working over any problems that might need to be addressed. Yet somehow he managed to be completely present in the moment.

Right now, however, he studied her with an intensity that made her feel as if he could read right through her. She hoped that he couldn't tell what she'd been thinking about from her expressions. He was a lawman after all, and it was his job to read people.

She straightened in her seat. "You startled me," she finally said.

The corner of his mouth quirked into a smile. "You looked so pretty sitting there that I didn't want to disturb you."

Heat rose to her cheeks. She didn't know how to respond to his compliment so she said, "I just finished setting up press coverage for the Halloween party and I was about to see if I could set a date for the debate with Chad's office."

"Why don't you save that for tomorrow?" Mike leaned forward and braced his arms on his thighs as he focused on her. "I have other plans for you."

She looked at him in surprise. "Oh?"

He gave a nod and got to his feet. "I'm going to steal you away from here. But first we need to stop by your place so you can change into jeans and sturdy shoes that you don't mind getting a little dirty."

She raised her brows. "What in the world do you have planned?"

He grinned. "A surprise, if you're game."

His grin was infections and she pushed back her chair. "Sure. I'm game."

Mike went to the restroom to change out of his uniform and into jeans and a western shirt. When he returned, she slipped on her blazer and grabbed her purse. They said goodbye to Megan, who was the only other person currently in the office.

It was brisk outside, the cool air chilling Anna's cheeks as they headed toward his SUV. He put his uniform onto the back seat and then helped her into the vehicle. He walked around the SUV, got in on the driver's side, and moments later they were headed toward her home.

She saw the babysitter, Carmen's, car parked out front when she reached the house. Anna knew her aunt and uncle would be at work, so she wasn't worried about running into them. She didn't know how they would react if they saw the sheriff in their home, and she didn't want to make them nervous. Not to mention her own tension would ratchet even higher.

Anna unlocked the front door with her key and opened it. The babysitter was the first person Anna saw and she said, "Hi, Carmen."

"Hello, Miss Anna." Carmen spoke with a strong Hispanic accent.

Josie came running in from the direction of the kitchen, Pablo following at a more reserved pace. "Anna!" Josie said and hugged her.

Anna smiled at Pablo who smiled back. He wanted so badly to be a little man that it was hard for him to be the boy he was.

Carmen nodded to Mike. "How are you, Sheriff McBride?"

While Mike greeted Carmen and the kids, Anna hurried to her room and changed into jeans and a long-sleeved T-shirt along with sturdy shoes. She put her wallet and keys into a smaller purse then grabbed a jacket that would be warmer for the evening.

When she was ready, she headed out to the living room. In moments they'd all said their goodbyes and Mike and Anna were outside, headed toward his SUV.

As he helped her into the vehicle, she thought about how easily she agreed to him taking her somewhere. She kept telling herself she needed to keep her distance and then she turned around and was off with him again.

"Are you going to let me in on where we're going now?" she asked him once they were headed out of town.

He flashed her a grin. "We're going riding."

"Horses?" She straightened in her seat and she couldn't help a burst of childlike excitement. "You're taking me horseback riding?"

He gave a nod. "Yep."

"Wow." She grinned. "I've always wanted to do that." She looked out at the highway as they started to leave Prescott. "And I get to see your ranch. Double bonus."

Their conversation was animated, just as it had been on their way to the pumpkin festival. He made her laugh with his teasing and a few jokes. He was so enjoyable to be around that it was easy to forget anything negative that was going on in her life.

Not much later, they reached the ranch. "This is fantastic." She looked at the home, the barn and other outbuildings, and the corrals. She saw some cattle in one field and two horses in a corral.

She turned to Mike. "Are those the horses we'll be riding?"

"One of them." He nodded in the direction of a barn. "I just bought a mare, Dancer, from a cousin of mine." He glanced at Anna. "You met Jayson that night at Nectars."

"I remember," she said.

"I'd like to get better acquainted with Dancer." Mike drove the SUV over a cattle guard, and the vehicle vibrated. "So I'll be riding her."

"The one I'll be riding is gentle, right?" Anna asked hesitantly.

"Very gentle." Mike drove the truck up to the house and parked in front of it. "I'll show you around before we take a little ride."

"All right." Anna started to open the passenger door but Mike was there to open it for her before she had a chance to.

When she was out of the truck, they headed toward the house that had a rustic feel to it. It was a sprawling single-level ranch-style slump block home surrounded by mature cottonwood and oak trees. Bushes bordered the outside of the enclosed front porch that shaded a couple of large wood rocking chairs beside the front door.

They walked up a rock path that led to the porch and Mike unlocked and opened the screen door that was made from iron scrollwork in a western design. The screen door opened smoothly and silently. He held it for her as she stepped past him and she walked through the front door.

Once they were in the house and he had closed the door behind them, Anna paused a moment to take in his home. It was bright and sunny with big windows and open wood blinds. The floor was done in large tiles and throw rugs were scattered throughout the room. The place looked spotless, without dust on the surfaces of the entryway, coffee, and end tables, not to mention the cubbies in the entertainment center.

"I love your home." Anna moved across the large living room to examine some of the artwork. Western scenes done in watercolors or pencil hung on the walls. On many of the rooms surfaces were bronze sculptures that reminded her of Remingtons but were clearly by a different artist.

Mike came up from behind Anna. "My cousin, Clint's, wife is a sculptor."

"They're wonderful." Anna smiled up at him. "She's incredibly talented."

"She sure is." Mike nodded in the direction of an archway. "We need to take water with us and a snack if you're hungry."

"A snack sounds good." Through the archway she could see a kitchen done in stainless steel and beautiful black and brown mottled granite. "I forgot to eat lunch. When I get busy, I lose track of time."

"Can't have that." He looked at her and shook his head. "We'll eat lunch now. You don't need to be lightheaded while riding. Do you like egg salad sandwiches?"

"Love them." She followed him into the spacious kitchen.

Cheyenne McCray

He opened the refrigerator door. "One or two?"

She leaned up against the kitchen island. "One is more than enough for me."

He proceeded to make three egg salad sandwiches from eggs he'd already boiled. He cut the sandwiches in half and put them on a big plate. In the meantime, after he pointed out where everything was, Anna put a couple of luncheon plates and napkins on the table, along with two glasses of iced tea. He grabbed a big bag of barbeque chips and carried the bag and the plate of sandwiches to the table.

They sat and Anna thought they were the best egg salad sandwiches she'd ever had. They chatted as they ate, much like they had in the truck when they'd been on the way to his ranch.

She faltered a little when the thought of Chad crossed her mind, but she managed to recover without Mike suspecting anything.

When they finished their sandwiches, Mike took a package of pecan shortbread cookies out of the pantry and offered some to Anna. She ate three before she told Mike that she was more than full.

"I'm ready to ride," she said as she cleared the table and he helped.

When they finished, he grabbed two large water bottles from the fridge and they headed outside toward the barn.

CHAPTER 12

Mike brought the horse Anna was supposed to ride from the corral, and her insides gave a little twist. The horse was so big and she'd never been around horses before now.

"Anna, meet Zinnia." He held the horse's halter while stroking her forehead with his free hand as he spoke to her. "Zinnia, this is Anna." He smiled at Anna as he moved his hand from the horse and dug into his pocket. He brought out some large green pellets. "Why don't you feed her these? I promise she won't bite."

Anna held out her palm and Mike dropped a few pellets onto it. She tentatively held out her hand to Zinnia and almost jerked it back when the mare lowered her head and her nose touched Anna's palm. At first Anna stiffened but then she relaxed as the horse snuffled over her hand. Zinnia's nose felt like velvet. When the horse raised her head, the pellets were gone.

"Go ahead and get to know her." Mike stroked Zinnia's neck and Anna followed suit and lightly touched the mare. "Horses like to be talked to."

Anna cleared her throat. "How are you doing, Zinnia?"

"I'll get her saddle." Mike held out the rope that was clipped onto the mare's halter and Anna took it. "Zinnia won't go anywhere, but go ahead and hold on to the lead."

Anna tried not to show her nerves as she gripped the rope and nodded to Mike. "We'll be waiting."

She continued stroking the mare that was dark brown with white socks and a white blaze on her forehead. "You are a beautiful girl. Sure you won't mind me riding you?" Zinnia bobbed her head up and down as if in answer, and Anna smiled. "Okay, but I'm putting a lot of faith in you and Mike." Zinnia whickered and looked at Anna with big brown eyes that appeared so sincere that it made Anna wonder just how much the horse understood her. "You really are a doll, aren't you?"

Mike returned, carrying a horse blanket and a saddle. He set the saddle on a nearby hay bale before draping the blanket over the horse. When he'd adjusted the blanket, he put the saddle onto Zinnia's back and cinched it on securely. The horse was so darn tall. Anna blew out her breath. It would be a long fall if she didn't manage to hang on.

She pushed that thought right out of her mind. She was *not* going to fall off the horse. She hoped.

When Zinnia was saddled, Mike headed back into the barn while Anna spent time with Zinnia, hoping that would cure her nerves over riding the horse. This time Mike took longer to return.

When he finally did, he brought a saddled horse out of the barn. The horse was another beauty, like Zinnia, but was completely reddish brown with no white. Mike brought the horse up to Zinnia and Anna.

"This is Dancer." Mike patted the horse. "According to Jayson, she has a good disposition but sometimes she's a little headstrong. I need to get to know her and she needs to get to know me."

Anna decided not to pet Dancer in case being headstrong meant being on the aggressive side.

Mike picked up the two large water bottles, and put them into one of the pair of saddlebags that were draped over Dancer.

"I need to adjust the stirrups for your height." He eyed Anna then took care of the stirrup on the right side of Zinnia before the left. When he finished, he faced Anna. "Ready?"

She looked at the saddled horse and back to Mike. Her stomach clenched a little again but she nodded. "I think so."

"You'll enjoy riding once we get going." He beckoned her closer. "Always get on the left side of the horse, putting your left foot in the stirrup and then swinging your right leg over her back."

As he moved close to Anna to boost her up, she felt a steadying of her nerves just by his presence. But when she was in the saddle she felt suddenly out of control, her skin prickling.

"It's such a long way to the ground." She swallowed as she looked down and tensed as the horse shifted beneath her. "And she's so big."

Mike rested his palm on her thigh and it warmed her through. "You'll be fine, Anna."

She gave a tentative smile. "I've always wanted to ride. This is my chance."

"I'm going lead you around a bit and give you some direction," he said. "Once you're sure you're comfortable, we'll go for a ride."

She nodded, grateful he wasn't taking her immediately out for a ride. "I think that's a great idea."

He led Zinnia around the huge yard while Anna clenched her fingers in a death grip on the saddle horn.

"Take a deep breath and try to relax, honey." He brought the horse to a stop and placed his hand on her thigh. "She can sense your nervousness."

Anna did as he told her to and inhaled through her nose before letting her breath out through her mouth. She repeated it as she loosened her muscles and her grip on the saddle horn.

"That's better." He gave her a gentle smile and moved his hand from her thigh. "Let's try this again." He patiently led the horse around the yard as Anna continued to breathe in and out slowly and concentrated on relaxing.

After another ten minutes, he halted the horse. "Now why don't you try your hand at the reins?"

She started to tense again but reminded herself to relax. She took the reins and Zinnia looked over her shoulder at Anna with her soulful brown eyes, as if to say, "I've got you."

"I can do this," she told herself as much as she was saying it to Mike.

He gave her a smile. "Yes, you can." He instructed her on how to hold the reins, how to get Zinnia to go, how to guide her in the direction she needed to go, and how to bring the horse to a halt.

They spent a good fifteen minutes allowing her to get used to handling the reins before he asked, "Are you ready?"

"Yes." She nodded and let out her breath. "As ready as I'll ever get."

Mike mounted Dancer and Anna felt her belly tip now that he wasn't guiding her or the horse.

He brought his horse up beside hers. "We're going on an easy ride." He gestured toward a pasture. "Flat, easy to traverse." He gave her a teasing smile. "We'll save the jumps for next time."

"Ha. Ha." She shook her head but smiled. "Let's go. I'm ready."

"Good girl." Mike made a clicking sound with his tongue and Dancer started forward.

Zinnia didn't take any prodding. She fell into step beside Dancer and Anna's heart rate kicked up a bit. They were off and going on her first horse ride. Her nervousness turned into enjoyment as they continued forward. Her body rocked with Zinnia's slow and easy gait.

They rounded a corral and came to a stop at a fence. Mike swung down from Dancer and opened up a gate before leading the horses through, Zinnia keeping up at Dancer's side. After the gate was closed, Mike mounted his horse again and they headed along the fence line inside the pasture.

Anna looked at him and the relaxed way he sat in his saddle and tried to follow his example.

"I have to warn you." He met her gaze. "You'll probably be sore as hell tomorrow."

She raised a brow. "As in having-difficulty-walking sore?"

He gave a low chuckle. "That's pretty safe to say."

"It'll be worth it." She looked around her at the dry yellow grass and at the clear blue sky. The air was crisp but her light jacket kept her warm enough that she only felt the chill on her cheeks and her hands as she gripped the reins. She met his gaze. "It's a gorgeous day."

"Yep." His horse sidestepped what looked like a large gopher hole. "Can't get much nicer than this."

The ride was slow and relaxing and it wasn't long before Anna didn't feel like such a novice at horseback riding.

"What was it like growing up with three brothers?" Anna asked. "I don't have any siblings."

Mike shrugged. "John and I were alone with Dad for the first several years before he married Angel. It took some time for us to get to know her and accept that we had a new mom and new brothers."

"I can see how that would be difficult." Anna stared off into the distance, thinking about her own parents and how much she missed them.

"What about your family?" Mike asked. "Is it just your aunt, uncle, and cousins?"

"Here in the U.S." It wasn't going to hurt to tell Mike about her other family. "My parents passed away just a few years ago but I have other relatives in Mexico City."

Throughout the ride Mike told her about growing up on a ranch and some of the things he and his brothers would do. He talked about his cousins who'd been rodeo champions and his cousin who was a world champion bull rider. Mike had such an easy, likable way about him that she enjoyed listening to the sound of his voice, the inflection, and the way he told stories.

He made it easy to forget she was on the back of a large beast, far enough off the ground that she could fall and it would no doubt hurt like hell. She found herself more than enjoying the ride. She felt almost high, exhilarated and on top of the world.

After they had stopped at a watering hole Mike had played in with his brothers as a kid, he looked at Anna and gave her a smile. "Let's head on back now."

She nodded. "All right."

During the journey back, the conversation turned from family to his campaign, and she asked him some questions that had occurred to her. Mike didn't seem overly focused on the bid for re-election. Maybe it was just that he didn't want to talk too much about it on what might be considered another date.

When they returned to the ranch, she had enjoyed herself so much that she couldn't stop smiling. It was hard to believe they'd been gone for a good two and a half hours and it was almost evening.

"Thank you." She waited as Mike swung down from his seat on Dancer's back. "What an incredible day."

He grasped Zinnia's halter with one hand and rested his other on her thigh. "I'm glad you enjoyed yourself. I sure enjoyed the time with you."

She smiled and put her hand over his that was on her thigh. "I loved it."

"Good." He grasped her and helped her down so that her feet touched the ground. He kept his hands on her waist for a long moment as he looked into her eyes. She had the feeling he was going to kiss her, but he let his hands slide away. "We'll do it again some time."

She felt a sense of disappointment but shoved it aside. As far as spending more time with him, she didn't want to think too far into the future so she simply smiled and said, "Yes."

As they started to walk back into the barn, she took a step and winced. "I'm already saddle-sore. I can't imagine what tomorrow is going to be like."

He paused to rub her shoulder and gave her a teasing look. "If you'd like a massage, just let me know. I'd be more than happy to oblige."

Heat rose to her cheeks as she couldn't help visualizing Mike massaging her aching leg muscles, especially her inner thighs. Thoughts like that led her into a territory she shouldn't be thinking about whatsoever.

He winked and they continued on to the barn while Anna tried to recover from her embarrassment.

She was anxious to get out of the flirting danger zone. "Is there anything I can do to help?" she asked when they reached the cool interior of the barn.

He proceeded to remove Zinnia's saddle and set it on a hay bale. "I've got it."

She sat on a hay bale and watched as he removed the saddlebags from Dancer and then the saddle.

"I'll brush Zinnia and Dancer down after I take you to Prescott." He took Dancer by the halter. "First I'll get these girls in their stalls and then drive you back to town and your car."

As soon as Mike had the horses back in their stalls, he returned to Anna and she dusted hay off the seat of her jeans. They walked to his SUV, and once they were in the vehicle and ready to go, they headed back into Prescott.

When they arrived back at the campaign office, and Mike had helped her out of the SUV, he walked her to her car. It was dusk and the streetlights had just come on, and they walked companionably in silence.

They reached her car and she unlocked it. She turned to tell Mike "thank you," when he took her off-guard by taking her face in his hands and lowering his mouth to hers.

She was mesmerized by the look in his eyes, by the feel of his hands on her face, by the heat of his body close to hers. He paused and waited a moment, his mouth hovering over hers.

Her entire body was still except for her heart that pounded like crazy. He brought his mouth to hers and her world seemed to spin. He kissed her long and slow, as if they had all the time in the world, as if nothing existed but the two of them.

Nothing mattered but his mouth and his tongue as he tasted her and she tasted him. A sigh escaped her and he slid one hand down to her lower back and pressed her close to him so that she felt the entire length of his body against hers.

She almost moaned, wanting more of him than she should. A part of her wanted him more than anything she could imagine. Another part of her knew that wasn't possible.

Yet she couldn't get herself to break the kiss.

Mike raised his head. Her lips parted, her heart still beating like crazy as she looked up at him.

She finally found her voice. "Thank you for today." It came out in a near whisper.

He stroked her hair and tucked it behind her ear. "Thank you for going with me. I like being with you."

Her throat worked as she swallowed. The words came out before she could stop them. "I like being with you, too."

He smiled and touched the corner of her mouth. "You are a special woman, Anna. I'm glad you came into my life."

His words sent a little shockwave through her that reminded her of all the reasons why this was wrong. Chad, her family…not wanting to break his heart.

"I'd better go." Her lips trembled as she forced a smile. "I need to help my aunt cook dinner."

He studied her a moment and she felt as if he could see deep inside her, deeper than anyone ever had before. "Are you coming to the office tomorrow?"

She gave a nod, feeling some relief at the change of subject. "Yes. I have to arrange the debate and the meet and greet." She shifted her stance but he still hadn't let her go. "I talked with your Aunt Gert today and set up the Halloween party press coverage."

"That's good," Mike said.

Anna found herself smiling. "She's probably your biggest fan."

He smiled, too, and she could see his genuine fondness. "I think you're probably right about that. Gert is a hell of a woman. She's always been good to me. She's always treated my brothers and me like we're her own."

"My aunt is like that," Anna said. "She's been like a mother to me."

Mike tweaked a lock of Anna's hair. "I'd better let you get on home so that you can help your aunt with dinner."

"It's tamale night." Anna took a step back and Mike let his hands slide away from her waist. "Thank you again."

"Any time. And I mean that." He gave her one more quick kiss before holding her car door open for her.

When she was inside, he shut the door and waited for her until she'd backed up and pulled her car onto the street. She looked in her rearview mirror to see him still watching her drive away.

CHAPTER 13

Mike rubbed his chin as he stood in front of the one-way glass. He watched as Reg Schmidt interviewed Jaime Nuñez. The man was one of Jesus Perez's men who'd been brought in for questioning regarding the murder of a young woman, Beth Franco, who'd been close to Perez.

Beth had recently turned informant when she'd overheard Perez talking about murder and human trafficking. The sheriff's office had arranged to have her wear a wire tonight—but now she was dead.

Reg was a hard man who didn't have a hell of a lot of tolerance. He saw the world in black and white, no gray areas, which had its good and bad points when it came to doing his job as a law enforcement officer. If Reg suspected someone, the person was guilty until proven innocent. Reg had been a sergeant when Mike took office. Frankly, he wouldn't have hired the hothead, much less promoted him to sergeant, if it had been his choice.

Right now Reg was attempting to verbally beat down Nuñez, who was sitting in his chair wearing a smirk. Mike folded his arms across his chest as he watched. Reg's face was getting redder by the moment. Mike frowned. The deputy looked close to losing control.

Betty Turner came up next to Mike. She was frowning, too. "Reg is going to pop a vein if he keeps this up."

Mike turned his gaze on Betty. "Get in there and see if you can get anything out of Nuñez before Reg—"

"Holy crap." Betty darted past Mike to jerk open the door to the interrogation room.

Mike whirled to see Reg holding Nuñez by the throat with one hand while he pounded his fist into Nuñez's face.

"Shit." Mike ducked into the room on Betty's heels.

Betty grabbed Reg by one arm while Mike gripped his other. Reg's face was livid, having gone from red to purple.

"Let me at the fucker." Reg fought against Mike and Betty's holds and he almost got out of Betty's grip. "He killed that girl!"

Nuñez was bleeding, but he was grinning through the blood.

Another deputy charged into the interrogation room as Betty and Mike dragged Reg out. The deputy was Ernie Walters, a long-time veteran of the sheriff's department. Ernie made sure Nuñez wasn't going anywhere as Reg was removed.

Reg stopped fighting and Mike slammed the door behind them once they were out of the room.

Mike ground his teeth as he fought back his temper. He rounded on Reg. "What the hell was that?"

Reg snarled. "The sonofabitch was practically bragging that he'd done it. You know he killed Beth Franco."

"In my office." Mike narrowed his gaze at Reg. "Now."

Mike turned and fought down his anger as he strode into his office and moved behind his desk, but remained standing.

Reg walked in behind him, his face still purplish red, his knuckles red from hitting Nuñez, and blood on his sleeve.

"Close the door," Mike said in a hard tone.

The deputy did so and turned on Mike. "The bastard deserved it."

Mike locked eyes with Reg. "Sit down."

Reg looked like he was going to argue but he parked his ass in one of the two chairs in front of Mike's desk.

"This isn't the first time you've lost control." Mike remained standing but bent slightly, bracing his palms flat on his desk. "This time you've forced my hand. I'm writing you up."

"What?" Reg's face turned purple again. "That fucker—"

Mike cut him off. "Next time you will be suspended."

Reg's jaw dropped. "You can't do that."

"The hell I can't." Mike seated himself in his office chair. "You've been a loose cannon since I came into office. This is something I should have done long ago."

The deputy gripped the arms of his chair. "You're too damned soft on these shitheads."

"You're going to want to watch your mouth." Mike gave him a long hard look. "I won't warn you again. I can and will fire you if I believe you're a danger to this office." He nodded to the door. "Take the rest of the day off."

Reg bared his teeth but pushed himself out of his chair. He glared at Mike and looked like he was going to fire off something else but instead he pivoted, jerked open the office door, and stormed out.

When the deputy was gone, Mike leaned back in his chair, his jaw tight. He dragged his hand down his face. If it came down to it, he'd have no problem firing Reg. The man wasn't worth having around with the trouble he caused. With the crap he'd been pulling, he was going to get the sheriff's department sued.

Mike turned to his desktop computer and started to log on when a knock came from the direction of the door. He turned his gaze on the open doorway to see Anna knocking on the doorframe.

She bit her lower lip when she saw his face. "Sorry to disturb you," she said before he had a chance to say anything. "I noticed it's a little hectic in your office."

Just the sight of her caused some of the tension to drain out of him. "You could never disturb me." He gestured for her. "Come on in and have a seat."

"I stopped at Sweet Things to get some doughnuts for the campaign office. While I was there, I bought you a couple of treats." She hesitantly held up a pink bakery box as she took a step into his office. "Although you look like you could use a drink rather than an éclair."

He couldn't help a low chuckle. "I'm on duty so I'll take the éclair."

She seemed to relax and she took the seat that Reg had just been sitting in. She was definitely a sight better to see in that chair than Reg was.

With a little smile she set the box on the desk. "I don't want to bother you while you're working, so I won't stay. I need to get to the campaign office soon, too."

He settled back in his chair and took her in, trying to avoid letting her see his gaze take in the red cowl neck sweater she wore that hugged her body and was drawn snugly across her breasts. Her long dark hung over her shoulders and alongside her breasts as well as falling in dark curls down her back.

"You're the best thing to happen to this office all day."

"That rough, huh?" She glanced over her shoulder at the doorway.

Through the doorway he saw Betty and Ernie talking with another deputy. Since she'd noticed things were a little crazy, he wondered if she'd overheard the deputies talking about what had just happened. Did he need to have a conversation with them about their professionalism when civilians were in the office? He'd have to say something just to make sure.

She returned her gaze to Mike. "I'm going to work on setting up the debate today. As long as Chad agrees to it, we should be able to have it the week before Halloween."

Mike smiled. "Perfect."

He watched as she tucked hair behind her ear, and he had a strong desire to be the one touching her hair, her face—

"Sedona is having a fall festival on Saturday." Her words brought him back to reality. "I thought that might be a good opportunity to get out and meet the public. The arts, music, a barbeque, and other events."

"I've gone in the past." He gave a nod. "They put together a hell of an event."

"Great." She leaned forward in her seat. "Once I get these set up, you'll have to think of other things I can do for you."

He could think of a few things she could do for him, none of which were suitable suggestions for public appearances, much less mentionable. He mentally shook his head. This was no way to be thinking about a lady like Anna, but that was easier said than done. She was so damned beautiful. Kissable. Touchable...

With a nod, he said, "I'm sure we can find something for you to do."

She got to her feet. "I'd better get to headquarters."

"Thanks for the éclair," he said as he stood, too.

She gave an impish smile. "Next time I'll stop by with a bottle of whiskey."

He grinned as he came around the desk to where she stood. "Believe me, if I was a drinking man, today would be a perfect time for it."

"I hope your day gets better," she said as they moved toward his office door.

He never liked to think of challenges as more than just that. "I wouldn't say it's a bad day. Just a little challenging this morning."

Her smile broadened. "That's the way I like to think, too."

He nodded toward the exit. "I'll walk you out to your car."

"Thanks." She fell into step beside him.

They headed toward the front entrance together and outside. Her car was parked a short distance away, in front of the YCSO.

The day was windy and overcast and Anna hugged her arms around her body. "I should have worn my blazer."

Mike would have put his arm around her shoulders but they reached the car and there hadn't been a real opportunity to do so. She pressed the button to unlock her car and he opened the driver's side door for her.

"If today doesn't get out of hand, I'll stop by the campaign office," he said. *Any more out of hand than it already has.*

She put her hand on the door and smiled at him. "Then maybe I'll see you later."

He touched the base of her spine and she stilled. He lowered his mouth and moved his lips over hers for a long slow kiss. She sighed and kissed him in return.

When he drew back, her face was flushed, her eyes glittered with desire and he had no doubt she wanted him as much as he wanted her.

He let his hand slide away from her lower back and she noticeably relaxed, as if the sexual tension of the moment had dissipated.

She slid into her seat and he closed the door behind her.

Anna let out her breath as she pulled away from the curb and drove away as Mike walked back into the sheriff's office.

As she headed back to the campaign HQ, her phone rang. She didn't recognize the number. She pressed the connect button and put it on speaker phone before answering with, "Hello."

"Anna." Chad's voice caused a crawling sensation down her spine. "I saw your car parked outside the sheriff's office."

Her skin tingled with irritation. "What do you want?" The moment she said the words she regretted snapping at him. It wouldn't do to tick him off.

"I don't think that's any way to respond to someone who holds your future in his hands," Chad said, his tone suddenly hard. "What did you learn while you were at his office?"

She tried to keep her tone even without emotion. "Nothing. It was busy so I didn't stay long and Mike was probably preoccupied with one of his deputies."

"Why was he preoccupied with his deputy?" Chad asked.

Distracted by a streetlight turning red ahead of her, she said, "I heard a couple of other deputies say that someone named Reg lost control in an interrogation." The moments she said the words, she wished she could take them back.

"Reg lost control?" Chad said with clear interest in his voice. "In what way?"

Her throat worked as the light turned green. "I—I'm sure it was nothing."

"How did he lose control?" This time Chad's words were harder and held a note of warning.

"He beat up some guy named Nuñez, I think, that they'd brought in for questioning." She swallowed as she drove on, hoping she hadn't just screwed up big-time by saying something that could hurt Mike.

"What else?" Chad asked and she didn't like the nasty sound of his question as he said it.

"Just that it wasn't the first time." Anna wished desperately that she hadn't answered the phone. She felt trapped and unable to get out of her current situation. "One of the deputies said that Reg has a short fuse. The deputy said it had happened it before, that he'd hit a suspect, and that it had only been a matter of time before he really lost it. The deputy also said that he should have been written up long ago."

"Thank you, Anna." This time she heard a note of satisfaction. "You've finally been of some use. Just make sure you keep your senses sharp and get me all of the information you can on Mike. Understand?"

Anna's stomach turned over and she felt sick inside. "Yes."

"Good." Chad disconnected the call without another word.

"Damn." The word did nothing to express how she really felt. She felt used and guilty for using Mike to keep her own secrets from being revealed.

She bit her lower lip and struggled to hold back tears as she drove through traffic.

This was all wrong, so very wrong. She was going to hurt Mike and she didn't know what to do about it. Once the election was over and Chad couldn't hold her family over her head anymore, she'd have to pull away from Mike. There was nothing else she could do, no other choice she could make.

No way out.

CHAPTER 14

Mike placed the phone back in its cradle and started to dial his assistant, Clarice, who'd attempted to get through to him twice.

"Sheriff." Betty's voice sounded urgent as she rushed through the doorway into his office. "Turn on the news."

Mike frowned at the concern in the deputy's tone. He picked up the remote from his desktop and pointed it at the flat screen TV in the corner of his office. The TV came to life and a news anchor was talking, while behind him was a picture of Reg next to one of Nuñez, which had been clearly taken after his release. His lip was split, his eye swollen and black, and his nose looked broken.

In the next moment, a recording of Nuñez being interviewed flashed onto the screen. "He went crazy on me," Nuñez said. "I didn't do nothin' wrong."

The camera went back to the anchor. "According to our source, Sergeant Schmidt has been known to abuse other suspects."

It was only a day after Mike had reprimanded Reg, and shit had just hit the fan.

Mike clenched the piece of paper he'd been holding. "What the hell—"

"The sheriff has allegedly been negligent in writing up the deputy," the anchor added. "Channel 7 news attempted to reach Sheriff Mike McBride but he was unavailable for comment."

Mike dropped the piece of paper on his desk and dragged his hand down his face. That was no doubt why Clarice had buzzed his office while he'd been talking with one of the informants on Jesus Perez. He hadn't asked the informant to hold because he'd been lucky to manage to get the man to talk to begin with.

In the next moment a reporter was talking with Chad Johnson. "What kind of sheriff can't control his own deputies?" he said.

"What a dick," Betty said in a growl.

Mike looked at her. "How did this get out?"

She shook her head. "No idea, Sheriff. They sure as hell didn't hear it from me."

"I doubt they heard it from Reg," Mike said, more to himself. "Nuñez could have gone to the news about the beating, but the inside information had to come from someone on staff here."

That knowledge surprised him. He had a good relationship with the staff and the deputies. Reg was the exception, but he wouldn't have gone to the news about something that could get him in deep shit, which this just had. He'd have to go ahead and suspend Reg.

Mike blew out his breath. "Is Reg in the office?"

Betty nodded. "He looked ready to blow a gasket when his picture came up on the news."

Mike glanced at the TV, pointed the remote at it, turning it off before he looked back at Betty. "Send him in."

"Sure thing, Sheriff." She turned and left the office.

A short time later, Reg stormed into the office. "How did the news get that information?" he shouted.

Mike gave Reg a hard look. "You'd better settle down before I end up having to fire your ass now."

Reg sucked in his breath like he was holding back another bellow. His face turned purplish-red.

"An investigation will be made into your misconduct," Mike said steadily as he stared down Reg. "You'll be lucky if you don't lose your job over this." Mike leaned back in his chair. "You are suspended until further notice."

Reg balled his hands into fists. "What the fuck—"

Mike cut him off. "It'll be without pay if you say another word."

Reg's mouth clamped shut but his eyes burned with the fire of the words he had to hold back. He hesitated one moment and started to turn.

"Leave your gun and your badge," Mike said.

Reg whirled back to face Mike, his eyes bulging. His hands clenched and unclenched before he took his gun out of its holster and laid it on Mike's desktop. He unpinned his badge from his shirt and dropped it beside the gun. Without another word, he turned and marched out of the office.

Mike watched Reg leave before putting the deputy's badge and weapon in a drawer and locking them both inside it.

Damn. Mike considered everyone in his office. Who the hell could have leaked the story? He slowly shook his head. It had to have been a conversation that was overheard. It was the only answer that he could come up with.

He pushed his fingers through his hair as he worked through the problem in his mind. He'd have to call a meeting and make it clear to his staff that no department business was to be discussed outside the office or with anyone not employed by the department. It wasn't a conversation he should have to have with his staff.

His thoughts drifted to when Anna was in the office. He'd considered the need to talk with Betty and Ernie about discussing sensitive events when anyone was nearby in the office.

He wouldn't even consider the possibility that Anna could have mentioned it to someone. However, someone else could have overheard Betty and Ernie in the office.

Mike clenched his jaws. He was just going to have to put out this fire and put it out in a hurry. And that meant he was going to have to respond directly to the news station.

His desk phone rang and on the caller ID screen he saw that it was Clarice. He blew out his breath and picked up the receiver. "I'll bet you've got someone from the news on the line."

"Yes," Clarice said. "I've got Paige Windhaven from Channel 7 News." Clarice sounded apologetic. "Sorry, Sheriff. I tried to get through to you earlier."

"Thank you, Clarice," he said as he picked up a pen with his free hand. "Put her through."

* * * * *

Anna stared in horror at the TV in the campaign office. Chad had done it. He'd taken what she had told him and used it against Mike.

Her stomach clenched and she felt like she was going to vomit.

"Damn." Angel's voice came from beside Anna. "This is not good."

Anna couldn't speak and just stared mutely at the TV.

Megan moved into view. "That lowlife, Nuñez, must have gone to the news station."

"But how could they know about Reg's propensity for abuse?" Angel shook her head. "That's insider information."

"Things leak out," Megan said. "Someone could have overheard."

"Maybe." Angel's lips were tight. "Chad Johnson has to be behind this."

Megan nodded. "No doubt."

"Looks like we have some work to do." Angel put her hands on her slim hips. She looked at Anna, who still hadn't been able to speak. "Don't worry, sweetie. Mike will pull through this."

"Yes." Anna finally was able to get words out. "Yes, he will." And she'd do whatever she could to see that he did.

"Back to work for me." Angel turned and headed to her desk.

"Me, too," Megan said.

Anna returned to her desk, too, her skin prickling. That bastard, Chad. But what else had she expected from him?

Yesterday she hadn't been able to get hold of Chad's camp to arrange the debate. Now it would look like Mike would want to get a chance to respond to the accusations publicly with Chad. Anna hoped Mike would be able to recover easily from it.

She made some calls and finally reached Chad's campaign manager and offered a few dates that Mike was available for a debate. The man said he'd get back to her, but he was certain that one day during the week before Halloween would work.

He eventually called back and they set the date for a Wednesday, a week and a half before Halloween

When she was finished, Anna asked Angel what she could do to help and Angel gave her a couple of tasks to take care of.

It was nearing the end of the day when Anna started to pack up to leave. She stood as she shoved her phone into her purse, her mind filled with what she'd done to Mike. Her skin prickled. She was being watched.

She looked up to see Mike standing in the entryway to the office. He was watching her. At first she thought he must be thinking that she was the one who had to have leaked the information regarding the deputy beating the man he had in for questioning.

But Mike's lips curved into a sensual smile as his gaze met hers. For a long moment she was lost in the depth of sensuality that was clear in his eyes.

"Hi, Mike." Megan's voice jerked Anna's attention away from Mike. "How's it going?"

Anna was grateful for the interruption. She was afraid he'd see the guilt written on her expression.

"About as well as it can after today's news bomb," Mike said with a shake of his head. "How're you doing today, Meg?"

"I'm doing well." She picked up a backpack and swung it over her shoulder. She kept her laptop in the backpack along with her purse and other things. "Sorry for having to deal with that crap. We'll pull through, though. We're all confident."

"Definitely," Angel said from her desk. "We'll make sure you win this election."

"Hi, Mom." Mike went to Angel and bent to kiss her cheek. "Need me for anything?"

Angel shook her head. "We've got it covered."

"See you all tomorrow," Megan said, and everyone responded in kind.

After Megan took her leave, Mike went to Anna's desk where she'd stood, unable to move.

"Are you taking off?" Mike said, and she nodded. "If I'm not needed for anything, I'll head out with you."

"All right." Her voice sounded small but she worked up a smile.

They said their goodbyes to Angel and walked outside.

"Want to get a bite to eat?" he asked.

"I can't." She gave him an apologetic look. "I need to get home. My aunt and uncle both work late tonight and I said I'd relieve the sitter, watch the kids, and take care of dinner."

"When we go to the festival in Sedona on Saturday," Mike said as they reached her car, "how about we have dinner afterward?"

"Okay," she said before her brain caught up with her mouth.

He brought her against him and kissed her. "I could really get used to this," he murmured as he raised his head.

She could too…*almost.* "Good night."

He smiled and once again he was left behind, watching her drive away.

But this time as she drove away, a tear rolled down her cheek. She didn't know how long she could do this. Her heart was aching from hurting Mike through Chad.

The tear was because she knew the truth. She was falling in love with Mike, destroying her own heart while possibly destroying Mike's career.

CHAPTER 15

The sky was gray and overcast on Saturday and Anna checked the news to see if it might rain during the event in Sedona. Channel 7's weather forecaster said it shouldn't rain until evening, so Anna was hopeful that would be the case.

Anna had done some shopping at a great boutique in Sedona, which was one of her favorite places to shop. She and Chandra had made a few Sedona shopping trips in the past and had always come back with armloads of packages. She still hadn't heard from Chandra and the thought made her insides hurt. She missed her friend terribly.

Before Mike arrived, Anna took a long shower then dressed in a black silk blouse and black skirt that reached mid-thigh, and added a black blazer. She wore red heels and carried a red handbag to give her wardrobe a little pop of color. After applying her makeup, she let her dark brown hair fall in long soft waves around her shoulders. She added touches of gold jewelry at her ears and throat.

She prepared to keep things a little cooler between her and Mike when he picked her up. She needed some distance. This was business—she was helping him with his campaign.

However, once she was in the SUV with him, she couldn't do it. He was easy to be with and she enjoyed his company so very much. It was the same as it had been every time they'd spent time alone like this—he made her smile, laugh, and simply made her feel good.

The event was fun although cool, so she was glad for her blazer. She hung back while Mike talked with people and shook hands. A few individuals threw questions at him regarding the ordeal with Sergeant Schmidt. Every time someone brought it up to Mike, she felt a sickness in her gut.

Toward evening she was feeling tired and a little drained. Her face hurt from smiling, her feet hurt from walking, and her heart hurt from what she was doing to Mike and from knowing she'd fallen hard for him.

"I made a reservation for dinner at one of my favorite Sedona resorts," Mike said as they walked to his SUV. "I think you'll enjoy it."

She smiled. "I'm sure I will."

Once they were on their way to the resort, she sank into the seat and relaxed for the first time since they'd driven to Sedona this morning. She and Mike chatted about the day and by the time they reached the resort she was feeling better.

It wasn't long before they were seated and had their menus. Mike selected a bottle of Chardonnay from a local winery called Oak Creek Vineyards. The liquid went down easily and warmed Anna's belly. It had been a long time since they'd had something for lunch and she was starving.

Dinner was terrific. They had caprese salad for an appetizer, citrus-crusted salmon for dinner, and a flourless chocolate cake with raspberry coulis for dessert.

She wondered if they'd ever run out of things to talk about because they talked and talked without any lulls in the conversation. She was getting deft at turning conversation away from specifics about her family. She did talk about her own childhood and growing up in the small town of Bisbee with her parents. She told him how her aunt and uncle had come to live with her family while she was away at the University of Arizona in Tucson. She returned when her parents were killed to be with her aunt and uncle and cousins.

By the end of dinner, she realized she'd had far too much wine. The waiter had brought a second bottle and kept refilling her glass and Mike's, and she hadn't kept track of how many she'd had. Three? She wasn't much of a drinker, usually stopping at two glasses. Her face felt warm and she felt a tad bit dizzy as she finished her last glass of wine.

When they finished dinner, they left and walked toward the lobby. People were walking into the resort, soaked from rain, or carrying umbrellas that were dripping onto the stone-tiled floor.

"It's a mess out there," one man was saying to another. "Can't see five feet in front of you."

"According to the forecast, it's only going to get worse," another man said.

Anna looked at Mike who looked at her. "Since the weather is so bad, why don't we stay the night here?" Mike asked. Her cheeks flushed with heat, but he added, "Separate rooms, of course."

She hoped her face hadn't turned red. "That sounds like a good idea."

Mike walked toward the reservations desk and she fell into step beside him. His legs were so long that she had to walk faster just to keep up. He seemed to realize that he was walking a little too quickly for her and he shortened his strides.

While Mike arranged for the rooms, Anna stepped aside and called her aunt to let her know that she wouldn't be coming back tonight. Aunt Maria said she was glad to know that Anna wouldn't be driving back in the storm.

Once Mike had the keycards, they headed to their rooms that were across the hall from each other.

In the middle of the hallway, he took her by her shoulders and lowered his head, his face hovering above hers as their gazes held. So much was said in that long look. She saw a depth of emotion in his eyes that matched the feelings inside her.

Her throat felt thick and she could feel tears backing up behind her eyes. What was she doing to him? To herself?

She needed to think and she couldn't do so with him looking at her the way he was.

He brought his mouth to hers and kissed her long and slow. Her breath escaped her and she didn't think she could breathe again.

Hunger for him grew from deep inside and it was almost blinding in its intensity. When he finally raised his head, her breathing was fast, her heart pounding hard.

He brushed hair from the side of her face. "Good night, Anna," he said softly.

The ache in her throat made it difficult to swallow, but she managed. "Good night."

He took her keycard from her and opened her door before handing her the card again, and she gripped it tightly. She stood for a moment in the doorway as they looked at each other again before she slowly closed the door.

She turned, her back against the door as she stared up at the ceiling. The tears did fall this time as she felt the pain of her betrayal so intensely that she knew she could never forgive herself.

With a sob she slid down the door and hit the carpeted floor. She brought her knees to her chest and rested her forehead against her thighs and cried.

When her tears finally dried, Anna rested the back of her head against the door. She had come to the conclusion that she had to at least tell Mike that she was being blackmailed, and that it was her fault the incident with Reg Schmidt ended up on the news.

The only problem with that was she couldn't tell Mike why she was being blackmailed. She just needed to tell him she couldn't see him anymore.

But if she didn't do what Chad asked her to do, he'd let out that her aunt and uncle were here illegally, and Mike would be obligated to report it to the Border Patrol.

God, what a mess. Such a huge, horrible mess.

She stood and shrugged out of her black blazer and draped it over an armchair. She pulled her long dark hair back, tying it into a knot. After splashing cold water on her face and fixing her makeup, she straightened her spine, raised her chin, and headed toward the door. She almost forgot her keycard but grabbed it at the last minute.

The consequences of what she was about to do hit her hard when she let her door close behind her. She crossed the hall and stood outside of his door.

Deep breath in. Deep breath out.

She raised her hand. Hesitated. Knocked on his door.

Her heart beat faster. The click of the door being opened and then he was standing there, bigger than life.

She caught her breath. He wasn't wearing a shirt. She couldn't help looking over the expanse of his muscular chest, down his rippled abs to his Wranglers and belt, the only things he was wearing. His feet were bare, too.

Her gaze met his and she felt a heated flush of embarrassment when she saw the yearning in the depth of his brown eyes. He took her by her hand and drew her into his dimly lit room before closing the door behind her.

She dropped the keycard and it landed on the floor by her feet. Her pulse raced and her lips parted as she saw the hunger in his expression.

"I—" she started.

He braced one hand on the doorframe, caging her in so that her back was against the door. He was so close that she felt the heat of his body burning through her blouse and skirt.

"What are you doing here?" he murmured as his gaze focused on her lips.

She couldn't think. Why was she here? All she knew at that moment was that she wanted him to kiss her.

Her tongue darted out to touch her lower lip and she cleared her throat. "I need to tell you something."

He lowered his head and his mouth hovered over hers, his breath feathering over her lips. Before she could say another word, he kissed her.

And she was lost.

CHAPTER 16

Anna's mind spun. She couldn't think clearly. Mike's kiss sent her reeling even more out of control. She kissed him in return, bracing her palms on his chest, feeling his power through her touch.

She sensed his self-control was being tested and he was about to lose his tether on it. She wanted him to lose control...wanted him to take her. Make love to her.

Love. God, she loved him so much that she could think of nothing but how much he meant to her.

A low rumble rose from his chest and she felt the vibrations throughout her. He pressed himself against her, his denim-covered cock hard against her belly. He moved his lips from her mouth, across her cheek to her ear, and his stubble felt coarse against her skin.

"Anna," he murmured. She gasped as he nipped her earlobe, one of the most intense erogenous zones on her body. "So sweet."

The way he said the words caused butterflies to tickle her belly and she squirmed to get closer to him. The power in his hands sent more thrills through her as he moved his palms down her sides.

His strength in personality as well as his physical strength made her want him in ways she had never wanted a man before.

He slid his hands down, his touch burning her body, until he grasped her by her ass and picked her up. Her skirt slid up her thighs to her waist as she wrapped her legs around his hips.

She barely realized she was digging her fingernails into his back as he continued to touch her and pin her against the door with his big body. He shifted her and his erection pressed against her, only her silky black panties and his jeans keeping them apart. She wriggled, wanting to feel him more firmly against her and he moved his hips. She gasped at the feel of him rubbing against her silk-covered folds.

Inside her. *Now.* She had to have him, had to know what it would feel like to be joined completely with him. She wanted him to slide into her, stealing her breath and thought away as he took her.

Wrong. This is wrong.

No, it's right. So very right.

Nothing had ever felt more right in her life as his kiss, his touch, felt at this moment in time.

As she clung to him, her thighs around his hips, he leaned back just enough to unbutton her blouse. He handled the buttons deftly and then he had her blouse open and he cupped her breasts through the black satin bra.

His eyes met hers, passion burning in his gaze. "You are incredible, Anna." His voice was husky and filled with desire. "You are the strongest, most intelligent, sexiest, kindest woman I have ever met."

She swallowed as his gaze continued to hold hers. "Everything about you is amazing to me."

"You're the amazing one." He paused as he looked into her eyes, seeming to be waiting for something, waiting for her to tell him she wanted more, to tell him she wanted this as much as he did.

Her voice came out in a near whisper. "I want you."

And I love you, her mind added but she wasn't about to say the words aloud.

Still holding her with her legs wrapped around his hips, he carried her to the king-sized bed in the center of the room and set her on her feet on the floor.

He pushed her blouse over her shoulders and slid it down her arms. When it was off, he draped her blouse over a nearby chair before turning his attention back to her. He unfastened her bra, freeing her breasts before laying the bra over her blouse. "So damned beautiful," he murmured. She moaned as he lowered his head and slipped his warm mouth over her nipple.

"Please." She slid her fingers into his hair. She didn't know what she was begging for as he sucked each of her nipples, but she wanted it now. "Please, please, *please.*"

He raised his head and she moved her hands to his shoulders as he cupped her face in his palms. He lowered his mouth to hers and kissed her slowly, tenderly, taking his time instead of answering her with matching urgency. It was clear he wanted to draw this moment out, make it special for both of them.

She gave a little shudder of desire as he moved his hands down her shoulders to her waist, where he reached behind her and unzipped her skirt. The material slid over her bare legs and she stepped out of it, now only left in her black panties and red heels. He picked up the skirt and laid it over her other clothing.

"So sexy." He slid his fingers into her hair and released the knot she'd made in it before coming to his room. Her hair fell in long, loose waves over her shoulders and down her back. He nuzzled her hair and she heard him draw in his breath. "You smell incredible."

A gasp escaped her as he moved his hands to her breasts and fondled her nipples, rolling them between this thumbs and forefingers. She had a hard time breathing as her skin flushed hot and desire flowed through her core to every extremity. He set her senses on fire, and she felt like she might burn to cinders if he didn't satisfy the flames inside her.

He grasped the sides of her panties and he slid them down her body, guiding the panties with his hands until he was crouched in front of her. She trembled as he nuzzled the dark curls of her mound and she heard his inhale.

"You smell like heaven." He moved the panties down and she stepped out of them. She started to kick off her heels but he said, "Leave them. They're sexy as hell."

He rose up until he was standing over her. With the four-inch heels she was taller than normal and it was easier to reach up and kiss him as she wrapped her arms around his neck. His bare chest was warm as she rubbed her nipples against him. He was so big, tall, and solid, his body hard against hers, his jeans rough against the soft skin of her belly and legs.

She braced her palms on his pecs. Her hands trembled at first as she explored the muscular expanse of his upper body. So much steel beneath his skin. She'd never felt anything like his body. Excitement stirred in her veins, the desire to feel his weight on top of her.

His body radiated tension, as if he wanted to take her and toss her on the bed now instead of waiting. The thought made her heart beat faster. She was tempted to hurry and remove his jeans, but she forced herself to slow down. She wanted to explore him in every way that she could, to savor every moment they had together.

She moved her hands down his taut abs to his belt buckle. It took her a moment but she managed to unfasten his buckle before pulling the belt out of the loops. The buckle thumped on the floor as she tossed the belt aside.

Blood throbbed in her ears as she unfastened the top button of his Wranglers, and she felt the length of his erection against the jeans as she pulled the zipper down. She pushed his jeans over his hips and to the floor, and he stepped out of them. He picked up the Wranglers and pulled his wallet out before setting the jeans aside. From within the wallet he drew out a foil package and laid it and the wallet on the nightstand.

He wore boxer briefs that hugged his hips and stretched over his cock. She bit her lower lip, her body throbbing with desire as she traced the outline of his erection with her fingertips. He sucked in his breath and fisted his hands at his sides as if he was restraining himself from taking hold of her and taking control.

Holding her breath, she hooked her fingers in the waistband of his underwear and tugged down on the cloth, releasing his cock. She let out her breath and wrapped her fingers around his cock, feeling the soft skin over the rigidness of his erection.

She moved her hand up and down his shaft and rubbed her thumb over the head and spreading the beads of pre-come.

"Anna," he said with a note of warning in his voice. "My control isn't going to last much longer if you keep that up."

She smiled to herself before grasping his boxer briefs and pulling them over his hips as she lowered herself to push the underwear down to his bare feet. She knelt in front of him as she grasped his cock and started to slide her mouth over the hard length of him.

He caught her shoulders with his big hands and drew her up so that she was standing before him. He lowered his head and kissed her softly, moving his mouth over hers in a long, sweet kiss.

They stood with their bodies pressed together and it felt as if his body was growing hotter, burning her in sensual heat. He moved her until the backs of her thighs hit the mattress. He reached down and pulled the covers back before grasping her by her waist. He lifted her and laid her in the middle of the bed.

She looked up at him, thoughts going through her mind, all leading to how much she wanted him, cared for him...loved him.

He took the foil packet from the nightstand, opened it, and drew out the latex circle. He tossed the package aside before rolling the condom down his cock.

"Come to me." Knees bent, thighs wide, she held out her arms to him. "Please."

"You take my breath away." He eased onto the bed, pushing her knees farther apart as he knelt between her thighs. "Everything about you is special."

When he had shifted low enough, he pressed his lips to each of her knees, feather-light kisses that caused her to shiver with desire. He moved again so that he was now lower on the bed and he held her foot in his hand. He slipped off her heel and let it tumble to the floor. It tickled in the most delicious way as he kissed the arch of her foot. He trailed his lips up to the inside of her ankle and slowly made his way up to her knee. He darted his tongue out as he kissed her body.

Another rumble rose up in him. "You're so soft and you taste so good." He kissed her again. "I can't get enough of you."

She had grown so incredibly wet for him and she could barely wait for him to take his kisses even farther. She moaned and shifted on the bed, unable to control herself. Her legs trembled as he continued kissing her on her inner thigh to the soft skin between her thigh and her mound. He pressed his lips to her mound and she tensed, waiting for him to move lower.

Instead, he moved his mouth to the inside of her other thigh and trailed his lips up to her knee. He tested her control to the extreme as he grasped her other foot, removed her heel, and kissed her arch before making his way slowly back up again.

This time when his mouth touched her mound, he slid his hands under her ass, raising her a little. His broad shoulders pressed her thighs apart even more.

In the next moment, he went down on her, sending her mind reeling. She gave a combination of a cry and a sigh as he slid his tongue down the length of her folds. He made a sound of pleasure as he licked and sucked her soft flesh and she wriggled beneath him, unable to control herself as she made soft mewling sounds.

She reached for him and slid her hands into his hair and clenched the strands in her fists. That seemed to spur him on more and he treated her to him sliding two fingers into her channel. She gasped, unable to take her gaze off the man between her thighs.

An orgasm rolled toward her like a thunderstorm. White light flashed in her mind like lightning and her body trembled almost violently. A climax hit her with the strength of a hurricane. She threw her head back and cried out, gripping his hair even tighter in her clenched hands.

When he stopped she was out of breath as she came down from the peak she'd just tipped over. He rose up and she let her fingers slide from his hair. He eased up her body so that he was above her and he locked his gaze with hers.

"You look so beautiful when you climax." He ran his knuckles over her flushed cheek. "I could watch you for hours."

He lowered himself and braced his hands to either side of her waist. She gripped his upper arms, her fingers nearly digging into his biceps.

"There's so much I want to do to you." He studied her features. "For you. With you."

"Me, too," she said softly.

He reached between them and guided his erection to her folds. He moved his cock through her wetness, causing her to catch her breath as he rubbed her clit that was still sensitive from her orgasm.

"I don't want to wait." She squirmed beneath him. "I need you now."

His smile was pained yet sensual. He placed his cock at the entrance to her channel as he held her gaze. Slowly, he pushed his way inside her.

Her eyes flew open and she caught her breath as he slid deep within. He was so big that she didn't know if she could breathe again.

"You're so tight." He pushed himself all the way and her eyes widened from the feel of him stretching her and filling her so deep, like she'd never felt before. "And you're so wet."

She wriggled her hips. "Take me and don't stop."

He lowered his head and kissed her before rising again. He began moving in and out in a slow rhythm, and she gave a gasp followed by a sigh. It was a sound of pleasure, desire, and love.

His warm brown eyes never released her. He watched her as a heated flush traveled through her. Her skin tingled and she could feel an orgasm approaching at a steady pace. Her insides wound tight and a light sheen of perspiration covered her body.

The fierce expression on his face told her that he was close, too.

But then he stopped and pulled out. Her eyes widened. Before she could ask him why he'd stopped, he slid down the bed so that his mouth was over her mound again.

He ran his tongue over her folds and her body throbbed. He licked and sucked and made the rumbling noise that told her he loved going down on her.

"Mike." She panted out his name as she tried to maintain her grasp on reality. It slipped. "Oh, my—"

Her words were cut off as another climax hit her hard, seemingly out of nowhere, and she shouted from the sheer pleasure that was almost too much to take. Her core throbbed and her mind spun. The orgasm was intense in a different way from the first and it sent her senses reeling.

A droplet of sweat rolled along her hairline as she started to recover and come back to her senses. He eased back up her body and slid his cock inside her again.

He began thrusting, this time not at the same slow pace. She wrapped her thighs around his waist and raised her hips to meet him as he drove in and out. She slid her hands along his sides and dug her nails into his back as he took her harder.

The bed rocked against the wall as he drove inside and out. She could barely maintain her hold on the here and now, her mind threatening to fly away to oblivion. The two orgasms had taken so much out of her and yet she felt another one coming on. She'd never climaxed twice in one night before, much less three times. She had the vague thought that she might fly apart if she did come again.

He thrust harder and harder, his expression fierce, his jaw tight. She started to close her eyes when he said, "Look at me, Anna." His words were husky. "I want to watch you come again."

His words ignited more flames inside her and she felt like she was spinning out of control. This time she screamed when she came. It was too much. Too much pleasure. And it went on and on as he moved faster and harder.

He gave a grunt and a shout and she felt his cock throb inside her when he climaxed. His pace slowed and he moved in and out until he gave one last shudder. He pulled out and wrapped her in his arms as he rolled her onto her side on the bed.

They both breathed hard, their bodies slick with sweat. As they lay together, he trailed one finger down her cheek. "You look so beautiful right here with me."

She placed her hand against his chest, feeling his heart beat beneath her palm. "You are beautiful to me," she whispered. The words *"I love you"* threatened to come out but she managed to hold them back.

He shifted and ditched the condom in a wastebasket on the side of the bed and switched off the one light that had been on before pulling one sheet over them. She was so hot from their lovemaking that she was glad for the single sheet. He brought her into his arms so that her head was lying on his biceps, their bodies close.

She relaxed, closed her eyes, and listened as his breathing grew slow and steady and she knew that he was asleep.

When she opened her eyes, she watched him sleep and felt a longing, a yearning like she had never felt before. In the morning she might regret tonight, but at this moment she felt like this was where she belonged.

Even as she thought it, she knew it wasn't true. She did not belong here, she shouldn't be here.

"I'm sorry," she whispered, and a tear trickled down her cheek. "I should have told you instead of making love to you. When you find out—you will hate me."

He made a soft snoring sound as the words tumbled out of her mouth. "Chad has been blackmailing me to spy on you. He threatened my family and I felt like I had no choice. Not threatened in the way you might think, but in a way that would devastate us nevertheless."

It felt like a lump the size of a baseball had lodged in her throat. "It's my fault that the story of the deputy leaked out." She clenched her eyes tight and more tears squeezed out. "I didn't know Chad would do what he did, but the damage is done now. I should have known. Was I just being naïve or ignoring the obvious direction it would go?"

Her heart ached with so much love for him that it hurt to talk. "I don't know what to do. I feel lost. If I tell you the truth about my family, then you'll be obligated to do what you have to do. If I don't tell you…" She put the back of her hand to her mouth and choked back a sob. She lowered her hand and clenched her fist in the sheet. "If I don't tell you, I might keep harming you because I'm too scared to not do what Chad is blackmailing me to do. I wish I could tell you everything. I wish it would make everything all right."

For a long moment she watched him sleep, his features relaxed, his breathing still deep and even.

"I love you," she whispered then shook her head. "But I deserve your hate. I didn't deserve tonight."

Trying to hold back what were sure to be loud sobs, she slid out of his arms and off the bed. He stirred and her heart thumped as she froze. When she was sure he was still asleep, she moved again.

Darkness enveloped the room and she felt her way to the bathroom she opened the door a crack, slid her hand through the opening, and switched on the light so that she could see easier. With the slice of light to guide her, she gathered her clothing and dressed.

After she had slid into her heels, she picked up her keycard from where she'd dropped it then quietly opened the door and slipped out into the hallway.

CHAPTER 17

Mike shifted in bed and a smile curved the corner of his mouth as he thought about Anna and the incredible night they had shared. He rolled onto his side and put his arm out to wrap around her waist, but he touched nothing. The bed was empty.

He frowned and opened his eyes. The room was dim, the hotel blackout shades only allowing a sliver of sunlight through a gap. Her clothing was no longer draped over the chair—her clothes were gone. Had she left in the middle of the night?

The sheet fell to his lap as he sat up in bed and pushed his fingers through his hair. Thoughts of waking up with her in his bed had made him smile, but now he frowned. Did she regret their night? She might, but he was going to change that if it was the case.

He pulled the sheet aside and walked naked to the blackout shades and pulled them open so that muted sunlight came in through the sheer curtains and the room brightened. The sky was still overcast, but it wasn't raining. The room now lit well enough to see easily, he checked the bathroom to make sure she wasn't in there but it was empty.

His stomach rumbled. Once he was ready, he'd grab some breakfast and bring it to Anna's room. After he showered and tugged on yesterday's clothing, and stuffed his wallet and keycard into his pocket, he headed out of the room.

A continental breakfast was being served in the café. He piled a tray with more than enough for two—plates with cheese and cherry Danishes; banana nut, blueberry, and bran muffins; bagels with small ramekins of cream cheese; and a bowl of fresh fruit including purple grapes, sliced strawberries, chunks of pineapple, blueberries, and melon balls. He added to the tray two glasses of freshly squeezed orange juice and two cups of coffee with packages of sugar and little cups of half and half. He added two small plates and two rolls of silverware to the tray.

He made his way back to Anna's room and knocked on her door. A long moment of silence passed and he knocked again. "Anna, it's Mike."

A moment longer and the bolt lock *thunked* and the door mechanism clicked as the door opened. She stood barefoot in the open doorway wearing yesterday's blouse and skirt, but still managing to look fresh and unwrinkled. She had her hair pulled back again and looked absolutely beautiful, but he almost frowned at the redness in her eyes.

"Good morning, honey." He held up the tray. "Breakfast."

Her eyes widened almost imperceptibly in reaction to him calling her honey. "Good morning," she said in her voice that sounded slightly husky and he wondered if she'd been crying, and again he had to hold back a frown.

She stepped back and out of the way, and he paused to brush his lips over hers. Damn, she was so soft, so sweet. She caught her breath and he smiled.

It seemed as though he caused her to feel unbalanced and she didn't know how to act now that they'd made love. He wanted her to know that nothing had changed, and wanted her to know how much he cared for her.

He walked into her hotel room, noting the rumpled covers on the bed and her red purse sitting on a chair cushion. Her black blazer was draped over the back of the chair and her red high heels on the floor below. His thoughts turned to how sexy she'd looked wearing nothing but those heels and his groin tightened. He needed to push those thoughts right out of his head.

After he set the tray on a table, he set out all of the food and drinks before placing the empty tray aside on a nearby desk.

He pulled out a chair and gestured to it. "Time to get a little something in your stomach."

She walked toward him, suddenly looking shy as she reached him. Before she could sit down, he placed his palms on her waist, stopping her, and placed a soft kiss on her lips. He drew away and put his hands on the back of her chair and he pushed it in after she sat.

He sat in the chair beside her and took in the two empty plates in front of them along with the two sets of silverware rolled in napkins, before gesturing to the food. "Dig in."

"Thank you." She took a cheese Danish and set it on her plate, then speared pieces of pineapple and melon before depositing them on her plate, too.

He thought about asking her why she'd left, but had a feeling he'd make her uncomfortable if he did. Right now he wanted to make her feel comfortable with him even if it meant his question would go unanswered.

"Did you sleep well?" He took a bite of cherry Danish after asking the question.

"I slept okay." She stabbed a piece of pineapple on her plate. "I don't always sleep well in strange places."

"Sounds like you need a little fortification." He gestured to her plate. "Eat up."

She slid the piece of pineapple in her mouth and looked pleasantly surprised. "Sweet and juicy," she said after she swallowed.

The corner of his mouth curved. "Wait until you taste the Danishes."

He guided the conversation to safe subjects and she visibly relaxed. Something about last night had scared her in some way. He didn't know what it was, but eventually he would find out. He wasn't going to allow her to regret a moment they had shared together in his hotel room, much less push him away from her.

Normally she was talkative when they were together, but this morning she was more subdued. He eventually had her smiling, but she had put a wedge between them that hadn't been there before. It was his job to get rid of that wedge.

"Did you enjoy breakfast?" he asked when she leaned back in her chair and dabbed her napkin to her lips.

"Very much so." She placed her hand on her flat belly. "I am so full now that I probably won't need lunch."

He gave her an amused smile. "We'll see about that. You usually have a pretty good appetite."

She gave him a rueful look. "You're right, I do."

"I like that." He stood and took her by the hand and drew her to her feet. "It's nice to have a meal with someone who doesn't just pick at her food."

"Certainly no problem with me on that end," she said with a smile.

"No problems with you at all," he murmured, drawing her closer. "You are perfect."

A look passed over her face, like his words had sparked something inside her that meant the opposite, that there was some kind of problem inside that she was dwelling on. He didn't know what it could be, but for now he wanted to make her feel nothing but good about herself and about them. He didn't want her to regret one moment she'd shared with him.

He slid his hand to the small of her back, just above her ass. He cupped the back of her head with his other hand and lowered his mouth to hers.

Her throat worked. "I need to tell you something," she said, and it reminded him of last night when she'd said the same thing before he'd cut her off with a kiss.

He shook his head. "For now I want you to enjoy this moment. I want you to know how right this is."

Her lips parted as if to say something, but he captured her mouth with his, stealing away her words. She trembled slightly in his arms and at first her kiss was tentative. Within moments she was kissing him with a passion and a hunger that rivaled his own.

Need drove him and he started to unbutton her blouse as he kissed her. He wanted her naked and he wanted it now. When her blouse was unbuttoned, he pushed it over her shoulders and she let it drop to the floor.

This time he couldn't move slow, couldn't take his time. He needed her with an intensity that shook him to his core. He pulled down her bra, spilling her breasts into his hands. He tore his mouth from hers. "I've got to have you, Anna honey. I don't know if I can take it slow this time."

"I don't want it slow." She trembled in his arms, a tremble of excitement.

With a groan, he lowered his head to capture one of her nipples. She moaned as he sucked it and then she gave a gasp when he lightly bit her nipple. At the same time he pinched her opposite nipple. She clenched her hands in his hair as repeated the act when he moved his mouth to the other one.

He raised his head and she let her fingers slide from his hair. He toed off his boots and pulled off his socks before she reached for his buttons.

She seemed almost frantic as she unbuttoned his shirt and pulled it out of his jeans. He jerked it off and tossed it before he reached behind her and unzipped her skirt and let it slide down her thighs to the floor. He pushed her panties over her hips and let them drop, too, before taking off her bra and throwing it aside.

When she was naked, he pressed his body tightly to hers, loving the feel of her soft bare skin as he skimmed his palms over her flesh. "You feel so good in my arms," he said while thinking, *and I'm never going to let you go.*

She moved back a little and reached for his belt buckle. In moments she had it unbuckled and his zipper down, and was dragging his jeans and boxer briefs over his hips as she knelt before him. He stepped out of his jeans and was about to draw her back to her feet when she wrapped her fingers over his cock and slipped her mouth over it, taking him to the back of her throat.

His breath hissed through his teeth and he clenched his fists in her long dark hair. "Damn, Anna." A rumble vibrated his chest, as if a caged animal was trying to break free from inside him.

She moaned and sucked him harder as if having her hair pulled while going down on him was erotic to her. Feeling as if he held power over her at the same time she held power over him was a heady experience.

"That's so good. So damned good." His heart beat faster as he felt an orgasm freight-training its way toward him. Her mouth was so warm and wet and she took him as deeply as she could.

He was so close to climaxing, so close to losing control, that he almost came in her mouth. Before he tumbled over the precipice, he pulled his cock out of her mouth and grasped her by the upper arms. He drew her to her feet, swept her up in his embrace, and laid her on the bed.

"Please." She said the words urgently. "I want you inside me. Now."

"I will be, honey." It took him only a moment to fish a condom out of the wallet in his jeans pocket. He rolled it down his erection and he eased onto the bed, between her thighs. As much as he wanted to wait, he couldn't, especially with her begging him to hurry.

He positioned his cock at the entrance to her core before driving into her.

She gasped and her eyes flew open, her lips forming an O, as if having forgotten how big he was. He watched her, like he had last night, to make sure there was no pain in her expression. When he saw nothing but pleasure, he started thrusting in and out of her hard and fast.

"Yes," she said in a husky whisper. "Yes. More. Please." She raised her hips up to meet his as he fucked her.

I'm making love to her. Love.

Her lips were parted, her eyes heavy-lidded, and a sheen of perspiration coated her skin. His orgasm was so close that it was all he could do to hold back. He wanted her to climax before he did, wanted her to feel pleasure before he allowed himself to come.

"Mike." His name was a sultry gasp that rose up in her. "I—I'm so close."

"That's it, honey." He ground his teeth as the intensity of her words almost caused him to climax. "I want you to come. Come right now."

A cry escaped her as her body bucked and shuddered beneath him. Her core clenched around his cock and that sent him flying straight into one of the most powerful orgasms he'd ever felt. He thought last night's had been unbelievable and yet this one shook him to his bones.

His cock throbbed as he thrust in and out of her until he couldn't take it anymore. He pressed his groin tight against hers as he looked at her flushed face and stared into her deep brown eyes.

I love you, came to his mind and it took everything he had not to say those words. It was too soon and he didn't want to scare her away.

Instead, he pulled her into his arms and held her close, hoping that she could sense the depth of his caring through his actions.

Together they cuddled until their breathing slowed, and all he knew was that he never wanted to let her go.

CHAPTER 18

Anna thought she was going to go crazy during the hour plus drive from Sedona to Prescott. Mike seemed so relaxed and in such a great mood, even singing along with the radio, and she couldn't bring herself to crush that mood for now.

After their night and morning together, how could she say, "The sex was great and I'm in love with you. By the way, I have been lying to you by omission this whole time. I've given Chad ammunition to chip away at your credibility and my family is here from Mexico illegally. Please don't report them."

Her stomach twisted, a sick feeling deep in her gut. She thought she might vomit from the spinning of her thoughts and the ugliness she was immersed in.

The beauty of making love with Mike, the amazing way he had shown her a depth of caring she didn't deserve, was rapidly eating away at her.

Dear God, what am I supposed to do?

Mike coaxed her into conversation about the upcoming debate on Wednesday, and the event they had gone to yesterday. He had a knack of knowing what she didn't want to talk about, however, at one point he said, "Something's bothering you, Anna. Do you want to talk about it?"

She froze when he asked the question. This was the moment she should spill everything.

"Nothing." The lie didn't come easy, but it was all she could get out. "The event yesterday was long. I'm a little tired from it."

She was certain he didn't believe her, but he didn't press her. As he drove, she looked out at the rain-washed high desert and tried to corral her thoughts. They pinged and bounced everywhere and she couldn't seem to focus on any one thing.

When they finally reached Prescott, she breathed a sigh of relief. They reached her house with plenty of time for her to make the late morning mass. Her uncle's truck was parked in front of the house. A black Cadillac was across the street, a vehicle she didn't recognize as belonging to anyone who lived nearby. The neighbors must have company.

For a moment she was worried Mike would ask to go inside her home, but she circumvented it by saying, "I'd better hurry. We have to leave for church."

He nodded. "Glad we got back in time for you to go." He climbed out of the truck, went to the passenger side, and helped her out.

She bit the inside of her lower lip looked at him, feeling a whirlwind of emotions from love to need to sadness to guilt. The guilt obliterated everything else.

"I had a great time," she said as she tried to come up with more to say. But all she managed was a lame, "Thank you."

He cupped her face in his hands and brushed his lips over hers. "I'll call you this evening."

She nodded as he released her face before she turned and hurried up the sidewalk to the steps. Her heels clicked on the stone as she walked up them. When she reached her front door, she glanced over her shoulder to see him watching her. She managed a little wave before opening the door and let herself inside.

Tears threatened the backs of her eyes, but when her two young cousins rushed in, she put on a smile. They both hugged her and she squeezed them to her in return.

"Were you two good for your mom and dad?" she asked.

Five-year-old Josie nodded enthusiastically. "You wore that outfit yesterday."

Before Anna could respond, Pablo said, "That man who came to church is here to see you. He's in the kitchen with Mamá and Papá."

A cold chill rolled over her skin and she remembered the Cadillac parked across the street. *Chad.*

Chad walked into the living room from the kitchen. "Hi, Anna."

Her features froze. "What are you doing here?"

He smirked. "I had a nice talk with your aunt and uncle. They're very hospitable."

Anna turned to the kids. "Tell your mom and dad that I'll be back in just a moment and I'll hurry and get ready for church."

Josie nodded and darted from the living room to the kitchen. Pablo, on the other hand, looked from her to Chad and back.

He started to say something but Anna laid a hand on his shoulder. "Go on now."

With a frown, he turned and walked into the kitchen.

Anna opened the front door. "We'll talk out here."

She didn't wait for him and stepped out onto the porch. Anger combined with fear caused her body to tremble as he followed her out. She shut the door firmly behind them.

Chin raised, she folded her arms across her chest. "What are you doing here?" she repeated.

"Stopping by to see what you have for me." The smirk hadn't left his face. "Thought I'd say hello to Aunt Maria and Uncle Tito while I was waiting for you."

"Stay away from my family." She clenched her arms tighter against her chest. "Call me next time."

A dangerous glint sparked in his eyes. "You are not the one who gets to say how I contact you."

Her face flushed with heat and she ground her teeth. "I don't have anything to tell you that would interest you."

"Oh, I think you do have something that interests me considerably." He casually looked at the street where Mike had dropped her off and returned his gaze to hers. "You're fucking McBride."

The heat in her face traveled across every inch of her body. She uncrossed her arms and fisted her hands at her sides. "I just told you that I have nothing on Mike."

Chad narrowed his gaze. "You'd better or your aunt and uncle can kiss the American dream goodbye." The heat in her body turned to ice. He started to leave but paused. "I expect something from you by Wednesday morning."

He clearly wanted something on Mike for the debate that night.

She remained rigid as she stared after Chad and watched him walk out of her front yard, across the street, and to the Cadillac. He opened the door and climbed inside. She didn't move until he'd driven out of sight.

Tears rushed forward and down her cheeks. She put her hand over her mouth to cover her sobs. Everything slammed into her at once and her knees almost buckled. She sat down hard on a bench beside the front door and buried her face in her hands.

* * * * *

Anna had managed to avoid Mike for the past two days by claiming to be sick, and that she hadn't felt well enough to talk on the phone. But today was Wednesday and she needed to be at the debate tonight. She was counting on things being too busy to have to talk with him much.

It was early when she went into the campaign office. Angel was already there but Megan hadn't come in yet.

"How are you feeling?" Angel asked when Anna walked in.

"Much better." Anna still felt sick in her gut, but that wasn't exactly something she could share with Angel. Anna felt guilty for lying to Angel and Mike about being ill.

Anna went to her desk and busied herself, avoiding talking to Angel as much as she could. Today was the day that Chad had demanded she hand him something on Mike.

Maybe she should have come in and tried to find something on him to give to Chad, but she hadn't been able to get herself to do it. It made her sick to think about betraying Mike any more than she already had and at the same time she felt ill from the danger to her aunt and uncle.

She would just beg Chad for more time even though she had no intention of giving him any fuel against Mike. If she could put Chad off, maybe she'd be able to come up with some way out of this.

As she worked on last minute details on the debate, she came to a conclusion that she should have seriously considered days ago. She and her family needed to move somewhere they would be safe from Chad. Now she just needed to put him off.

A call came in on her cell phone at ten and she now recognized the number as Chad's. When she answered, he said, "What do you have for me, Anna?"

"I've been sick with a cold." She kept her voice low so that Angel wouldn't hear. "This is my first day back in the office. I need more time to find something for you."

"I told you today." His voice sounded harsh.

"I'm sorry." She swallowed, her mind racing. "Please give me another few days and I'll get what you want."

The long moment of silence that passed caused her stomach to twist. "All right," he finally said. "Take all the time you need."

He disconnected the call and Anna's skin prickled. How had he gone from demanding information for today and then telling her to take all the time she needed? What was he up to?

Maybe nothing. She set her mobile phone on the desktop as her mind whirled. Her phone rang again, startling her. She glanced at the screen to see that it was Mike. She couldn't talk to him now, not when she was feeling like she was going to crawl out of her skin, so she sent the call to voice mail.

She set about making sure all last minute preparations were ready for the debate tonight. She was determined to see Mike come through it with flying colors.

CHAPTER 19

Mike pulled his department SUV into the parking lot and turned off the ignition. For a long moment he stared at the town hall. Anna filled his thoughts and warmed him. He'd tried to call her but she hadn't been feeling well. Her voice had sounded thick, and she'd said she was coming down with a cold. Angel said Anna had made it to work today, but the day had been so damned busy that Mike hadn't had a chance to get over to the campaign office.

Despite his memories of his time spent with Anna, a deep feeling of unease had him off-balance. He wasn't sure why he felt as if the other shoe was about to drop. Maybe it had to do with Reg Schmidt, maybe not.

Still frowning, Mike climbed out of the SUV and shut the vehicle door before heading toward the town hall building. It was dark but still early enough that the parking lot was almost empty. Wouldn't be long before parking spaces would be difficult to find.

Unease had stayed with him all day and he couldn't shake it off. That wasn't like him and he wondered what was behind it. It couldn't be the debate—he'd never had a problem with nerves and he found it easy to talk about things he was passionate about.

When he got inside the building, he went backstage and ran into Angel.

"Are you ready?" Angel adjusted his tie and stepped back to look at him. "I was proud of the boy you were and I'm so very proud of the man you turned out to be."

Mike brought her into his arms and hugged her. "I think you're pretty special too, Mom."

Tingles slid down Mike's spine and he knew someone was behind him. Not unpleasant tingles at all. He kissed Angel on top of her head then stepped back with a smile before looking over his shoulder to see Anna.

Damn, just seeing her made his heart jerk hard. She was beautiful as always, but today she looked drawn and like something heavy was on her mind.

Angel squeezed his hands, drawing his attention back to her. "I've got some things to take care of. Knock 'em dead."

He gave her a grin. "Just for you."

She smiled and walked into the growing mass of people backstage.

Mike looked at Anna again and moved toward her. She looked nervous. When he reached her, he ran his knuckles along her chin and she visibly shivered.

"Everything all right, honey?" He settled his palms on her upper arms. "Are you over your cold?"

"I'm still a little sick." She put up her hands as if trying to keep some distance between them. "I don't want you to come down with this, too."

"Don't worry about me." He felt the heat of her body through her dress and wanted to press himself to her, wanted to feel her body against his.

She put her hands on his chest and pushed. "Please."

A quality was in her tone that made him frown. "What's wrong?"

"Nothing." She shook her head then pursed her lips. After a brief hesitation, she added, "I really need to talk with you after the debate."

He continued rubbing her arms through her dress sleeves. "I'll take you out to dinner."

She hesitated and he thought he saw longing in her eyes. "No. We need to talk someplace private."

"All right." He gave a slow nod, feeling a little puzzled. "We'll make it happen."

"Thanks." She reached into a black leather case attached to a strap that hung from her shoulder. She pulled out some papers and handed them to him. "Some things for you to go over."

He flipped through the pages then looked at Anna. Her gaze darted around the backstage that was growing denser and denser with the number of people. She went still and her features seemed pale.

When she looked back at Mike, she said, "I've got to go take care of a few things. I'll see you after the debate."

Before he could say anything, she was gone.

He'd never been one to feel so much uncertainty about something he cared deeply about, and he cared more for her than he was ready to admit.

Maybe he should admit it. Maybe he should tell her exactly what he thought and how he felt.

He was in love with her. Head over boot heels in love.

The thought caused his belly to pitch then settle. He felt a confidence about Anna that he'd never felt with anyone before. He couldn't imagine anything she had to tell him that could possibly change anything between them. Nothing short of murder.

By the time the debate was ready to start, the town hall was crowded and it was standing room only. Mike nodded to people he knew as he walked onto the stage. He walked across the stage and stood behind one podium while Chad stood behind the other. Mike normally felt comfortable with public speaking. Today felt off somehow, but he was still confident that he would be able to handle anything that came his way.

Mike looked into the audience and saw friends and other people he'd had interactions with over the years. Anna was sitting to his far left, in a seat next to the outside aisle. Her gaze met his and he started to smile at her but she quickly looked away.

He managed to hold back a frown. She hadn't returned his call today and they had only spoken briefly before he had to take the stage. Something was wrong beyond her having been sick for a few days. He had a hunch she was regretting their night and morning together.

Tonight, after the debate, he'd let her know how he felt about her. He wasn't going to let her pull away from him, not when he was certain she was as crazy about him as he was about her. He had seen it in her eyes, felt it in her touches. It had not been just about sex between the two of them. It had been far more.

The moderator, Sybil Renfrew, a Prescott councilwoman, lobbed the first question at Chad when the debate officially started. Sybil was tough but professional and Mike respected her.

As the debate progressed, Chad's expression grew more and more smug, making Mike wonder what the hell the man was up to. Chad claimed that the sheriff's department budget was not being handled correctly, that the jail system was in trouble, and that crime was on the rise.

Mike easily refuted all of Chad's accusations and in turn pointed out his opponent's lack of experience in law enforcement and in handling budgets on the scale of the sheriff's department.

When Sybil brought up the issue of illegal immigration, Chad's expression went serious, as if he was loath to give the information he was about to deliver.

"I don't want to mud sling, but it just isn't right and the constituents of Yavapai County should know the truth about a serious matter." He paused and hair prickled at Mike's nape. Chad continued, "Sheriff McBride is dating a woman, Anna Batista, who lives with and supports two illegal immigrants from Mexico, her aunt and uncle."

The room went totally silent and Mike's mind reeled. What in the hell was Chad up to? Anna couldn't—

Mike's gaze locked on Anna and he saw everything written on her features. Horror and fear had immobilized her and her face had a shocked expression.

Chad went on with a serious look. "It was my duty as a law-abiding citizen to make authorities aware of their illegal status. U.S. Border Patrol agents should be at her home now and will be arresting her aunt and uncle then deporting them back to Mexico."

Mike couldn't take his eyes off of Anna as terror filled her expression. She hesitated only a moment before she got up from her seat and fled out of the town hall.

The hall was suddenly in an uproar, people standing and shouting, but their words were incoherent beneath the buzzing in Mike's ears.

Chad continued, "Being the Yavapai County Sheriff requires someone with a strong awareness and the tenacity to take charge and make tough decisions when needed. That's what I had to do today."

"Sheriff," Sybil's voice broke through Mike's shock and he turned his attention to her. The exclamations in the room died down. "What is your response to your opponent's accusations?"

"I have no knowledge of the validity of Mr. Johnson's claim." But Mike had seen it on Anna's face as clearly as if she'd said the words aloud. His mind was nearly numb as he continued, "My office will be conducting an investigation."

Mike's focus was shaken and he had to fight to gain control of his emotions, to push aside the pain of Anna's deception and the shock of what was clearly the truth. It took everything he had to concentrate on the debate.

Afterward, he was besieged by reporters and constituents and he repeated over and over again that an investigation would take place immediately.

At the same time, he thought of the terror on Anna's face and it was like an icepick to his heart. Whatever he would go through now, what she would be facing was far worse.

* * * * *

Nothing seemed real as Anna drove faster than she ever had in her life as she sped to her neighborhood. Fury over what Chad had done churned with the fear of what was happening at this very moment. How could he have done this? All in the name of making his opponent look bad, he didn't care what lives he destroyed.

Damn that bastard! Damn him.

The moment she turned onto her street, she saw the flashing lights of Border Patrol and Prescott Police Department vehicles that were parked in front of her home.

Tires screeched as she brought the car to a hard stop in front of the house and hurried out of the vehicle. Not bothering to lock her door, she ran toward the front porch where her two young cousins were sitting on a step.

A police officer with a hard serious expression, who Anna recognized as Mike's brother, John, stopped her in her tracks. "Do you live here, Ms. Batista?" he asked.

"Yes." Tears burned at the backs of her eyes. "It's my home."

He gestured toward the children. "Are they yours?"

She looked at the kids who wore terrified expressions. "They are my cousins."

"I'm Agent Davies," a Border Patrol agent said as he cut in. "Are the children U.S. citizens?"

"Yes." Anna nodded. "They were born and raised in Arizona." She looked from the agent to John and back. "Please let me go to them."

John gave a nod. "You can see the kids, but you'll be taken in for questioning."

Anna bit her lower lip and hurried past John McBride and Agent Davies, straight for Josie and Pablo. The kids got up and hurried down the stairs to meet her on the sidewalk, and both threw their arms around her as she swept them into her embrace.

Josie pointed toward the Border Patrol SUVs. Her voice cracked as she spoke. "Where are they taking Mamá and Papá?"

Anna whirled to look at the vehicles and saw Aunt Maria and Uncle Tito in the back of one of the SUVs. Maria had tears on her cheeks but Tito looked stony-faced.

If it wasn't for the kids, Anna would have broken down. She wanted to sink to her knees on the sidewalk and cry. But her young cousins needed her now, needed her more than ever.

"We'll figure this out." Anna squeezed the kids with her arms around their shoulders as she looked from five-year-old Josie to eight-year-old Pablo, knowing the kids would be growing up far faster than they should have to. *"Ser fuerte para tus padres."* She paused. "Promise?"

"Yes, I promise we will be strong for Mamá and Papá," Pablo said, but his voice trembled.

Anna had to fight to keep her own voice steady. "I know you will." She turned her attention to the SUV that her aunt and uncle were sitting in. Through the window, Aunt Maria's gaze met Anna's. A look of relief crossed Maria's face. She was clearly relieved to see the kids with Anna.

With a knot in her throat, Anna sank to the bottom porch step, the kids to either side of her. She kept them close as her mind whirled. Within moments the SUV with her aunt and uncle was leaving. She blinked back tears as she watched the vehicle disappear around the corner.

She felt Josie shaking and she looked down to see the little girl's body trembling as tears rolled down her cheeks. "I want Mamá."

"I know." Anna lifted Josie into her lap and rocked the little girl. "I will do everything I can, sweetheart."

Deep inside, Anna knew there was nothing she could do to reunite the children with their parents while they were under eighteen years of age. That didn't mean she would give up, but she would be fighting a losing battle unless laws changed. Her aunt and uncle would be deported and Pablo and Josie would never be allowed to go with their parents because the children had been born in the U.S.

The courts had determined that men and women crossing the borders illegally knew that they were taking a chance by allowing their children to be born in the U.S. The courts believed that the illegal aliens had made their choice so they must face the consequences.

What family would choose to be torn apart like this?

Anger rose up in Anna's chest at Tito and Maria. When her aunt and uncle had entered the U.S., they had gambled the fate of their unborn children. A tear rolled down Anna's cheek. Her aunt and uncle had taken a chance and it had just torn their family in two.

Anna held Pablo and Josie close to her, never wanting to let them go. Their family as they'd known it would be no more. Now Anna would have to fight to keep her cousins out of the foster system. She would do whatever was necessary to fight for custody so that she could raise the children herself.

Depending on what happened next, this could be her last chance to let the kids know how much she loved them.

Fighting to hold back tears, she swallowed as she kissed Josie's head and then Pablo's. "I love you," she said to each of them. "Your mother and father love you, too. Never, ever forget that."

Pablo continued to stare in the direction the SUV had gone with their parents. Josie buried her face against Anna's blazer and sobbed.

An image of Mike came to Anna's mind and the stunned expression he'd worn when his gaze had met hers in the town hall. She had never dreamed it would turn out the way it had, that Chad would set her up to use her against Mike in this way. If it had occurred to her in the slightest, she would have told Mike from the start.

The moment Chad had approached and threatened her, she should have moved her family. They could have been gone overnight, just taking what they needed. Mike wouldn't have been hurt emotionally or professionally by her situation. She wouldn't have betrayed him in the way she had.

Now there was nothing to be done for it but pick up the pieces and hope that Mike would one day find it in his heart to forgive her.

CHAPTER 20

Mike dragged his hand down his face as he leaned back in his office chair. The shitstorm that had come about after Chad's big reveal during the debate hadn't ended. It was a week after the debate and reporters and constituents still wanted to know how Mike hadn't been aware of the situation.

He ground his teeth. It would be unfair to even toy with the notion of checking the background of anyone who looked to be of Hispanic descent. It was racial profiling and it would be wrong.

Once he'd gotten over the initial shock, he'd remembered the times that Anna had tried to tell him something and how each time he'd distracted her and put it off. Had that been what she had been trying to tell him?

At the same time he wondered if she would have told him. She'd have known that no matter how he felt about her, he'd have had to report her aunt and uncle, no two ways around it.

He blew out his breath and looked up as a sound came from the doorway to his office. He looked up to see his stepmom, Angel, rapping on the doorframe.

"Can I see the sheriff?" she asked with a light smile on her lips.

"Anytime." He beckoned her in with a gesture as he stood. "What's going on with you today, Mom?"

"Getting ready for your Aunt Gert's Halloween party tomorrow night." Angel took the seat in front of his desk and crossed her legs at her knees as her warm hazel eyes met his gaze. Mike took his own seat again. "How are you holding up?"

The mention of the Halloween party brought his thoughts right back to Anna. She'd been the one to set up the event. He compartmentalized the thought for the time being. He was a logical man and he needed to be logical about the whole situation.

But what was the logical thing to do?

"Holding up just fine." He offered Angel a tired smile. "Once everything settles down we'll see how far I've dropped in the polls."

"Hopefully the storm will pass." She linked her fingers around her knee. "How is Anna?"

"I haven't spoken with her." He pushed his fingers through his hair. "Not for a lack of trying. She won't answer my calls and I haven't been able to get her alone."

Angel gave a slow nod. "How is it going with her fight to get the kids?"

"I've done everything I can to pull strings behind the scene." Mike picked up a pen and tapped it on his desk. "It hasn't been easy considering the part I played in the whole damn mess."

"I don't think Anna would have done anything to intentionally hurt you." Angel looked thoughtfully at him. "Although I don't understand why she would allow herself to become involved with an officer of the law in her situation."

Mike shook his head. "I pushed her."

"It takes two," Angel said quietly. "You can't blame yourself."

"Maybe I can." He glanced out the window. "She tried to tell me something but I brushed it aside. Who knows what it could have been."

Angel shifted in her seat. "How soon before Anna will know if the kids' guardianship will be awarded to her?"

"These things take time," Mike said, "But I'll do everything I can to help speed it along."

"Good." Angel tilted her head to the side. "What time will you arrive at the party tomorrow night?"

The thought of the ordeal the Halloween party might turn out to be not only for himself but his family members sat heavily on his mind. "I'll be there by six."

"Good," Angel said. "The media is supposed to be there at seven."

Mike wanted to groan but he managed to hold it back.

"Looks like Chad Johnson set up his own little Halloween party." Angel gave a small smile. "I say little, but he's planned quite the event and is inviting the most prominent people in the county and from around the state. That includes an Arizona state senator and a congressman, and, of course, the media."

"Can't say I'm surprised," Mike said. "The Johnsons enjoy throwing parties and inviting whomever they consider to be the current elite."

"That's putting it mildly." Angel shook her head. "Chad has always worked to one-up you since you were young. I imagine once he got word of the media showing up at Gert's, he had to create what he considers to be an even bigger event."

"Sounds like Chad." Mike's thoughts went to the smug look on Chad's face before he had dropped the bomb about Anna. Mike had thought of that smug look many times since the debate and every time he'd had the urge to knock that expression right off of the sonofabitch's face.

Chad hurting Anna in an effort to attack Mike was inexcusable. According to the law, Anna's aunt and uncle had to be reported. But it was the way Chad had done it that was so damned wrong.

Angel put her hands on the arms of the chair and a scowl crossed her pretty face, an expression that was rare for her. "That SOB is something else."

Mike raised an eyebrow. Angel rarely said anything negative about any individual, but it was clear she was upset with Chad.

"Yes, he's something else," Mike agreed.

"I'd better go." Angel got to her feet. "I've got more to do before the party."

Mike stood at the same time and moved around the desk to see her out. He kissed her cheek. "See you tomorrow night."

"Hang in there." She smiled and gave him a quick hug. "Everything is going to be fine. The people will see Chad for what he is."

Mike wasn't so sure about that, but he nodded and watched her leave. After she was gone, he went back around his desk and took his seat.

Anna, as always, came to mind—his thoughts never seemed to stray far from her. She might think he was angry with her, but he wasn't. He cared too damned much about her and saw her for the woman she was. She had been protecting her family, people she loved.

He picked up his phone and dialed her number once again.

* * * * *

It was the day before Halloween and Anna rubbed her eyes with her thumb and forefinger as she sat at the kitchen table with a mug of hot coffee. She moved both her hands around the mug, warming them as she stared into space.

The days had gone by like a nightmare. Maybe a part of her had known this whole situation was inevitable, but she had always hoped and prayed it would never come to pass.

Her aunt and uncle had come across the border illegally when Anna was in college and she hadn't had anything to do with them coming to live with her mother and father. Years had passed after Anna returned to Bisbee to live with them when her parents died, and her cousins had been born. Anna had grown accustomed to them being there.

It wasn't until they'd had to move from Bisbee to Prescott that Anna truly considered the danger. They'd come so close to her aunt and uncle being found out. What could have been done about it but move overnight? They had no options at that point. And now...

She shook her head. Now she had to see about getting health insurance for the kids and taking them to a counselor. She would have a lot more to work into her budget as the sole supporter of their little family. It put an end to her shopping sprees, but those weren't important. The only things that were important were her two young cousins, their wellbeing, and happiness.

"Hi, Anna." Josie's small voice captured Anna's attention as the girl walked into the kitchen.

"Hi, sweetie." Anna did her best to give her young cousin a smile. "Would you like a mug of hot chocolate?"

Expression solemn, Josie nodded and slid into the seat across from Anna. "Yes, thank you."

Anna scooted back her chair, went to the fridge, and grabbed the gallon jug of milk she had bought last night when she got the kids back.

Someone had to have intervened on her behalf for her to gain custody, even temporarily, this quickly. She had to work to get permanent custody of the children, but at least she had them now.

Anna poured milk into a saucepan and turned on the gas flame. While the milk started to heat, she went to the pantry and brought out a box of hot cocoa. She felt as if a great weight had been dropped on her shoulders and it overwhelmed her for a moment. How was she going to do this?

She looked over her shoulder. "Where is your brother?"

"He just went into the living room." Josie swung her legs as she sat in her chair, her legs too short for her feet to touch the floor. "He got out the X-Box."

It was too early in the morning for the kids to play games, but Anna just nodded. She had arranged to get Josie's and Pablo's homework assignments and she would have them do their work a little later.

Anna had decided not to make the children go back to school just yet—not after all of the turmoil and what the kids might face when they did go back. Prescott schools had a strict policy against bullying, but Anna was concerned that some of the kids might give Josie and Pablo a hard time when teachers were not around.

Not to mention she needed to give the children some time to grieve the loss of their parents. It would be almost like a death to them to not be able to be with their mother and father. Anna would do anything and everything to make the best of a beyond difficult situation.

Anna heated up enough milk for both kids and made two cups of hot cocoa. She set one mug in front of Josie. "Blow on it, sweetheart. It's a little hot."

After Josie had her mug, Anna went to the living room and saw Pablo sitting in front of the TV. Like Josie had said, Pablo was playing a game on the X-Box.

"I made a mug of hot chocolate for you," Anna said to him. "It's in the kitchen."

Pablo didn't look at her and continued playing the game. Her heart hurt for the boy. She didn't expect him to act like nothing had happened because his life had just been torn apart.

What was the best way to help the two children deal with this? She would make an appointment with a counselor as soon as possible, one who could help the three of them work through this.

She moved to the TV where Pablo was playing the game and sat on the carpet next to him. For a long moment she watched him play the game. He didn't look at her, his expression blank.

When he reached a stopping point, she picked up a controller. "Can I play, Pablo?"

He shrugged but set the game so that it allowed two players. Anna had played a couple of games with Pablo several times. She wasn't great at it, but she had always enjoyed the one-on-one time with him.

While they played, she didn't try to engage him in conversation because she sensed that he didn't want to talk. Just being there for him was what he needed right now.

Josie came into the room, chocolate on her upper lip, and Anna gave her a smile. Josie sat on the carpet so that Anna was between the children. After a while, Pablo seemed to loosen up a bit and Josie rested her head on Anna's shoulder, clearly needing the contact.

The overwhelming feeling that had weighted Anna down earlier lightened a bit. It wasn't going to be easy being an instant mother. She would do the best she could and do everything possible for the children that would allow them to deal with their grief. Children were resilient, but it would be some time before they were able to move on.

"Sing for me, Anna." Josie's small voice took Anna from her thoughts. "You always make me feel better when you sing."

Anna thought about it a moment then began singing Josie's favorite song from the movie *Frozen*. Pablo stopped playing and Anna stroked his hair. She was afraid he would leave the room, but he stayed as she sang three more songs before it was time for the children to go to bed.

Once the two were sleeping, Anna wandered back to her living room. Her thoughts turned for a moment to Mike and tears bit the backs of her eyes. He had called her a few times but she hadn't answered.

Her throat ached as a lump formed there. After what happened, and how she had deceived him, he must hate her. She couldn't imagine him wanting to see her.

Why had he called? To tell her how he felt? To ask why she had deceived him?

He deserved answers, but she wasn't ready to talk to him. How could she put it all into words? She wasn't sure she'd ever be able to talk with him again.

CHAPTER 21

Mike strode up the walkway to Aunt Gert's two-story home, in between painted Styrofoam gravestones, and skulls to either side. On the stairs, a skeleton shrouded in reaper's cloak and hood held a sickle and eerie noises came from beneath the hood. A severed head lay on a velvet cushion within a treasure chest near the front door and it opened its eyes and moaned as Mike walked by. Above the door was a massive web as well as a mechanical spider the size of a small child moving across the width of the web. Spooky music played from hidden speakers from the gate to the front porch.

Every year a team of adult family members, including Mike, helped Gert prepare for the Halloween party, and this year had been no different.

It was still early, before hordes of little and not so little witches, superheroes, cowboys, doctors, and princesses arrived. A lot of the adults who dropped by would also be dressed in costume.

Mike, who was in his sheriff's uniform, had stopped by to see if Gert needed anything else.

He rapped on the door with the heavy gargoyle doorknocker. Within moments a green-skinned witch with a long warty nose opened the door. Gert, dressed all in black, looked almost exactly like the wicked witch from the Wizard of Oz. She cackled, holding a broom in one hand, as she stepped back so that Mike could walk through the entrance.

She could almost be called a crazy cat lady with the number of cats she had—Mike thought at least ten prowled her house, but it was hard to tell. Right now one of her black cats twisted around her ankles that showed beneath her calf-length black dress. Mike wondered when she was going to start having flying monkeys as part of her Halloween decorations. It seemed she had everything else.

"Came early to see if there's anything else I can do for you, Aunt Gert," he said as she let him in and closed the door behind him.

"I think everything is taken care of Mikey, dear." She gestured to the surroundings, indicating all of the Halloween decorations, including ghost holograms and fog from dry ice just inches from the floor. The eerie sounds and music were piped into the house, too.

A skeletal "man" dressed like a butler in moth-eaten clothes was positioned by the front door and held a tray scattered with wicked spiders of all sizes. "I think we'll scare a few spitless," Gert said with clear delight. "Kids and adults."

He couldn't help a grin. "No doubt you're right."

"Would you like to eat?" She moved to the dining room and he followed.

Good things to eat—at least Mike hoped they were good—covered the extensive dining room table. The goodies included things like chips and pretzels beside black moldy-looking dip; crackers with cheese covered with black jelly; cakes shaped like headstones and skulls; bowls of candy; and green punch that frothed and spilled fog onto the table. Black paper plates, plastic ware, and cups were on a smaller table.

A loud rapping sound from the doorknocker came from the front door, followed by the doorbell ringing. Even the doorbell had been rigged so that a deep spooky voice answered.

"I need to get the door." With delight on her witchy features, Gert swept through the house to the front door. She opened the door with a cackle.

For the next hour, the doorbell and knocker sounded nearly non-stop. Mike grinned at the sight of kids dressed as wizards and witches, the Incredible Hulk, Iron Man, Thor, Spiderman, and more came through the door. One little girl was dressed up as a pink Darth Vader, and a boy wore an Iron Man helmet, big plastic Incredible Hulk fists, Spiderman tights, and a Superman cape.

Mike grinned when Megan and Ryan arrived with their three-year-old identical twin boys and two-year-old daughter. One of the boys was dressed as a construction worker, the other an astronaut, and the daughter was outfitted as a doctor.

Danica and Creed's three-year-old son was dressed as a superhero and Blake and Cat's newborn daughter wore a tiger jumper.

Mike found it amazing how fast the McBride clan was growing, from marriages to kids, including his own immediate family. Two of Mike's brothers were now married, and John and Hollie's wedding would be this December. Garret and Ricki of course had announced that they were pregnant with the baby due in the spring, and Angel was excited to be a grandmother.

As Mike watched the children at the party, his thoughts turned to Anna and her young cousins. The three of them should be out enjoying some trick-or-treating. Better yet, they should be here at the party. Mike had the feeling that after everything they'd been through, they weren't leaving the house for any kind of fun.

Thoughts of Anna made his gut tighten. Truth was he'd fallen hard for her, and no matter the situation, he cared for her too damned much to let her go. He was giving her time to become a mother to her cousins and for the three of them to adjust and come to terms with what their future held. But it was hard to be away from her...hard not to hear her voice.

Mike would track Anna down if he had to, in order to talk with her, but he wanted to make sure the timing was right. Everything in Anna's and the kids' lives had to be in complete upheaval right now.

As for Mike, he had an election to deal with and serving the people of Yavapai County was important. He'd spent his adult life working in law enforcement, dedicated to public service.

Mike didn't consider himself perfect by a long shot, but Chad was far from being the right person for the job. The way he'd callously announced Anna's situation in a public debate showed what kind of person he was. He was ruthless and had his own interests in mind.

That had always been the case with Chad. From the times they were kids, Chad had done whatever he could to serve himself.

Mike helped Gert keep the table loaded with food, cleaned up spills, and righted anything that was inadvertently knocked down or out of place. He generally kept an eye out to make sure everything went as smoothly as an event could with dozens of kids and teenagers running around in costumes.

"The news reporter is here." Gert came up from behind him as he set a refilled bowl of caramel popcorn on the table. "I'd like to meet her."

"Well, come on then." Mike smiled at Gert and gave her his arm.

Mike escorted Gert outside after she snatched a long black cape that went remarkably well with her witch costume. The night's biting cold made Mike grateful for his leather jacket as they exited the house.

"Sure you're warm enough, Aunt Gert?" Mike asked as they stepped onto the porch.

"Delightfully so." Gert beamed as she looked at the Channel 7 News reporter, Paige Windhaven, and her cameraman who stood on the walkway. The cameraman had his camera on and a light shone brightly, illuminating their faces. Gert's green-painted face looked even eerier in the lighting.

"Good evening, Ms. Windhaven." Mike held out his hand and took hers when he greeted her. "Welcome to the McBride family Halloween party, courtesy of our Aunt Gert." Mike gestured to his aunt. "Gert, this is Paige Windhaven."

Gert gave another witch's cackle and held out her hand. "I know who you are, dearie. I watch Channel 7 all the time."

"It's a pleasure to meet you." Paige gestured around them. "This is an amazing setup."

"Halloween is my favorite holiday." Gert gave a wicked laugh as she watched a pair of children dart past them. "The younger the kids, the juicier they are in my oven."

At the look on Paige's face, Mike almost choked on laughter. He managed to hold it back.

The reporter composed herself. "When we're finished with the interview, do you mind us taking a look around? I'd like to add some of the atmosphere of the party to the piece."

"Absolutely," Gert said with a nod.

"Do not film the faces of any kids who are not wearing masks." Mike was firm on that. Even though the reporters could get approval from the kids' parents, Mike would not allow it.

"Of course." Paige smiled. "We reviewed the requirements stipulated by Ms. Anna Batista when she set up the coverage." Mike felt himself grow hot under the collar as Paige went straight into the territory Mike had expressed he did not want to cover. "How could a campaign worker, the woman you're seeing, harbor illegal aliens without you knowing?"

Mike gave Paige a long, hard look. "It would be considered racial profiling to do a background check on any individual based on ethnicity. I do not believe in or support racial profiling."

Paige looked taken aback just for a second before she recovered. "I understand Ms. Batista is fighting for custody of the two children who are U.S. Citizens even though their parents were here illegally."

Mike's ears began to burn and he felt like his chest was on fire.

"Would you like a tour of the house?" Gert stepped in front of Mike. "I'll show you around."

"Yes, but—"

"Come along, dearie." Gert looped her arm in the reporter's and not so gently guided her up the front stairs. Gert glanced over her shoulder at the cameraman who was following with his camera focused on the backsides of Gert and Paige. "You're welcome to eat something while you're here," Gert said.

Despite Mike's anger at the reporter's questions, he almost smiled at the way Gert had swooped in to take over and protect one of her own.

Paige and her cameraman stayed for another thirty minutes, filming the extravagantly decorated home, kids who wore masks or the backsides of children who didn't, as well as filming adults in costume. Most of those in attendance were happy to support Mike's campaign. It was well known that the McBrides were a close-knit bunch.

When Paige turned to Mike one more time before walking out the door, she held her microphone up to Mike's face, "Sheriff, are you certain you don't want to comment on the situation with Ms. Batista?"

Before Mike could respond with something that wouldn't have put him in the best light, he heard a small scream and a gasping sound.

He whirled and saw Ricki with her hand to her neck, her face turning purple.

"Oh, my God," Paige said, but Mike was already rushing to his sister-in-law.

"She's choking." Megan sounded panicked. "Candy."

Mike grasped Ricki from behind, and using the Heimlich maneuver, he caused the piece of candy to dislodge from Ricki's throat.

The piece of candy flew out of Ricki's mouth and she would have collapsed to the floor if Mike hadn't been holding her. She coughed and wheezed as Garrett pushed through the crowd and pulled his wife into his arms.

The room had gone entirely silent.

"Honey." Garrett held Ricki close. "Are you all right? Is the baby all right?"

Ricki nodded but seemed to be having a hard time recovering her voice. "We're fine," she managed to get out. "Thank God for Mike."

"Thank you." Garrett looked at Mike. "I owe you." He put his hand to Ricki's belly. "We owe you."

Mike gripped his half-brother's shoulder. "You don't owe me a damned thing."

It was then that Mike heard Paige as she said, "There you have it, people. A demonstration of true heroism by our own Sheriff Mike McBride."

Mike whirled on Paige who pushed her microphone into Garrett's and Ricki's faces. Mike stepped in front of Paige as he pushed the microphone aside.

"She just about choked to death, Ms. Windhaven," Mike said, holding back his anger. "Give her some privacy." Trying to remain cool, he added. "I ask that you don't show that footage."

"Our watchers just saw it happen live," Paige said.

Mike rarely had to fight to control his anger, but he was finding it excruciatingly difficult to rein it in. Garrett appeared livid and Ricki looked mortified.

Paige, seeming to sense that she'd better leave while she could, said, "Thank you all for your hospitality." She looked nervously at Aunt Gert, who wielded a broom like she wanted to take out the cameraman. "We'll see our way out."

Mike thought he heard his aunt growl low in her throat and she looked menacing. "I'll walk you to the door," Gert said, her eyes narrowed.

Paige and her cameraman scuttled from the house with Gert holding the broom in both hands. When the front door closed, Gert returned.

She raised her hands, still holding the broom. "Lots more food is coming out of the kitchen. Come on, kiddos. Let's eat."

General cheering went up and the party fell back into full swing. Kids went back to running around, some chasing Gert's cats while some chased each other.

Mike was hugged multiple times by family members wanting to thank him for saving Ricki's life. Mike stopped arguing that anyone would have done it if he hadn't reached her first, as his protests seemed to fall on deaf ears. Angel was practically in tears as she squeezed him to her and thanked him for saving her daughter-in-law and future grandchild.

With a shake of his head, he thought about the incident being filmed. He was furious with Paige Windhaven for broadcasting Ricki almost choking to death, but there wasn't a damned thing he could do about it now.

When things died down and everyone appeared to be having fun again, Mike let out his breath. Ricki's moments of choking had scared the shit out of him, if he was being honest with himself. What if he hadn't been right there or if Ricki had been alone?

He knew better than to play what if games, so he pushed those thoughts aside. Instead he found himself thinking about Anna and what it would be like for her to be pregnant with their child. He thought about raising Pablo and Josie as his own and something in his chest lightened and loosened. They were good kids and he would be proud to raise them.

A big smile curved his lips as he pictured Anna with a swollen belly as they expected their first child. Yes, he and Anna would give them a young cousin or three to love, too.

It was not going to be easy for Josie and Pablo, for any of them for that matter, but as far as Mike was concerned, those kids would continue to know love as they had with their own parents. One day they would be reunited with their birth parents, but until that day, Mike would do everything in his power to make them happy.

CHAPTER 22

On Sunday, the afternoon following the Halloween party, Mike stood in his home office as he stared at his cell phone. He'd once again tried to reach Anna, but the call had gone straight to voice mail, just like all of the others.

Likely he needed to give her time, but he wanted to be there for her, to help her through everything she was going through now. He wanted to be there for her every step of the way, give her someone to lean on, and he wanted to give her his love. He missed her.

He would just have to go see her…but would the timing be right?

Damn but he couldn't stand staying away from her. It would take everything he had not to go to her home. For all he knew the kids could have seen him on TV and realized that he was a law enforcement officer and that might frighten them.

Time. He had to give them time.

His phone rang as he stared at it and he saw that it was dispatch. He answered the phone and was told there was an explosion and fire outside the Prescott town limits in an obscure area. It was suspected to be a meth lab that had gone up.

It didn't take Mike long to leave the ranch in the department SUV and hit the road with sirens and lights going.

When Mike reached the scene, the fire was still burning. Red and blue lights flashed from emergency vehicles that had arrived moments before Mike, including the fire department. It wasn't long before HAZMAT, more sheriffs' deputies, and ambulances were on the scene. Mike was informed that agents from the Drug Enforcement Agency were also on their way.

Deputies set up barricades the equivalent of a city block from the former meth lab, dangerous fumes keeping most emergency personnel at a distance. Those working near the meth house wore full-face respirators with supplied air.

"Sheriff." Betty Turner strode up to Mike. "We've got two men who claim to have been forced to work in the lab. They don't speak English and from our conversation, I've learned that they are UDAs."

Mike gave a nod. "Where are they?"

"This way, Sheriff." She jerked her head in the direction of an ambulance. "Border Patrol agents are on their way. Agent Davies indicated he was a couple minutes from here when he got the call, so I expect him to arrive any moment."

Mike strode with Betty along the outside edges of the perimeter. They reached an ambulance where two men sat on the ground as paramedics attended to them, treating their wounds and giving them oxygen.

Both men looked underfed, frightened, and dazed, with cuts on their hands and faces. However, they didn't look like meth addicts or act as if they had recently used the drug. It wasn't uncommon for individuals working in a meth lab to not be allowed to use the drug themselves.

Agent Davies from the U.S. Border Patrol approached Mike, along with a male and a female who wore badges on their belts. Mike guessed they were likely the DEA agents and he waited until Davies and the other two reached him.

Mike shook their hands and they introduced themselves. The DEA agent in charge was Leslie Wallace.

After the quick introductions, Betty looked from Davies to Mike and the two DEA agents as she launched into the explanation one of the men had given her. Their names were Kino and David, and they had been brought across the line with several other illegal immigrants.

Instead of gaining traditional employment, albeit illegally, Jesus Perez had forced the six Mexican nationals to live and work in the meth lab. Perez had starved them, treated them poorly, threatened their lives, and not one of them had been paid a single American dollar.

Mike moved in front of the two men. Kino was clearly in shock, and was still breathing in oxygen that paramedics had supplied. David took off his oxygen mask. He was beyond angry and spoke in non-stop in Spanish about what they'd been forced to do and to endure. It had been slavery, David shouted.

After Mike got David to calm a little, the man continued in Spanish, stating that Kino's wife had also been forced to work in the lab and was likely dead. David and Kino had been attending to something outside the house, behind a small structure, when the lab exploded. They'd received minor injuries while two women and two men in the house had probably perished.

The charred remains of the house smoldered as firefighters fought to put out the fire. Mike saw that two bodies had just been pulled from the wreckage and were being carried to the perimeter.

David went quiet as his gaze fell on the bodies and Kino stiffened beside him.

"Perez's threats are meaningless now," David said in Spanish as he stared out the bodies. "We will tell you whatever you want to know because we wish to avenge Kino's wife and our friends. Perez must pay for his crimes."

Mike nodded and asked questions. As he listened, his skin prickled, almost burning with every word David said.

"This is not the only meth house Perez has," David continued. "They have more in places like this where it is difficult for the police to find."

"Do you know where any other meth houses are?" Mike asked.

David frowned, quieting for the first time. It was clear that the man was turning the question over in his mind.

"One is five kilometers or more from here." Kino, who had been sitting by silently, took off his oxygen mask and spoke in broken English. "I have been there."

Mike straightened. "Can you show me how to get to the house?"

Kino's gaze riveted on the bodies, his jaw set, his eyes filled with tears. "That is my wife." Tears trickled down his soot-stained cheeks. He raised his hand and pointed at one of the bodies as it was covered. "Her shirt...she was wearing the red one today."

"I'm sorry for your loss," Mike said. A part of him hated to push a man who was so clearly filled with grief, but they had to act fast if there was even a chance they could catch Perez. "Can you help us find the other meth lab?" Mike asked. "We must find the man responsible for your wife's death."

Kino slowly nodded. "Yes."

Mike looked at Joe, one of the paramedics. "Unless there's a damned good reason why I shouldn't, I'm taking Kino on a little ride."

Joe glanced at Kino. "He doesn't appear to have sustained more than a few cuts and scrapes." He looked back at Mike. "He should be fine for a ride. Just make sure he gets to the hospital afterward for a thorough check up."

"You've got it," Mike said.

After he sent one of his deputies into town to get a warrant, Mike had a quick discussion with his deputies, Agent Wallace of the DEA, and Agent Davies of the Border Patrol. He then cuffed and escorted Kino to the YCSO SUV and put the man in the back of the vehicle.

With DEA and YCSO backup behind him, Mike drove from the meth lab as they headed further away from town into forested land. Sunlight filtered through the trees, the shadows across the highway growing long in the fading afternoon.

"Slow down," Kino said when Mike had driven almost seven miles and Mike reduced his speed. Kino leaned close. "It is there."

Mike glanced over his shoulder at Kino who held up his cuffed hands and nodded toward a rough dirt road that cut away from the highway into the forest. "That road."

Mike glanced to the road as he slowed the vehicle and looked at Kino. "You're sure?"

The man pointed to a twisted and gnarled black oak with a flat-topped boulder at its roots. "I remember that tree and that stone."

Mike pulled the SUV off the road and his backup did the same behind him. He climbed out and left Kino cuffed in the backseat. Mike walked to the back of the vehicle and opened it before putting on his vest and preparing for whatever they would face in the coming moments.

The early November air was crisp, cool, and smelled of the forest, a relief from the chemical-tinged air of the location they'd just left. Mike's blood pumped at a steady rhythm, warming him against the chill.

The DEA agents and Mike's deputies also put on their vests, strapping on leg holsters, taking additional ammo, AR-15 rifles, and whatever else they might need. They did everything quickly and efficiently. Mike and Agent Wallace worked together to plan their next steps.

In the meantime, the deputy who Mike had sent to town for the warrant called. He'd emailed a copy of the signed warrant to Mike's cell phone. Mike checked his email, saw the warrant, and they were ready to go.

From what they could tell, the pothole-filled dirt road was the sole egress to and from the house, and they blocked it off with vehicles.

Within a short amount of time, sheriff's deputies and DEA agents headed through the trees toward the house that was approximately two hundred yards from the highway. Two K9s accompanied them.

As quietly as possible, they worked their way to the home. Leaves crunched and twigs snapped beneath their shoes, making total silence impossible. But if there was no lookout and no one outside the building to hear, it wouldn't matter.

They reached the outskirts of a large clearing and Mike's pulse ramped up when he saw a gleaming red truck that he recognized as the same make and model as one belonging to Perez. They did a quick check on the license plate, and sure enough it was registered to Perez.

If they caught Perez now, they'd put the bastard away for a long time—if this was in fact a meth lab and they had the product on hand.

The house itself looked like it could fall apart at any moment. With its partially boarded-up windows, and walls that were weathered to a splintered dark brown, any hiker might have thought it was abandoned.

Damn, if this place went up it could easily cause a forest fire. The brush and trees were dry thanks to a meager monsoon season.

Nothing stirred. A moment later, a voice came from inside the house, breaking the silence. Someone barked orders in Spanish but the words were muffled and Mike couldn't make all of them out. The orders were followed by a loud crash and then a string of curse words in Spanish that were so loud Mike could hear those clearly.

The deputies and agents stayed at the tree line surrounding the large clearing. There would be no breaking down the door or charging into a meth lab. It was far too dangerous. The place could go with a single muzzle flash. If they had to, they would send in a drone. They'd prefer not to send in any of the K9s due to the danger that the place could explode.

When the house was surrounded at a good distance, Mike caught the familiar pungent odor that went with meth labs, akin to cat piss. He had no doubt they'd found exactly what they were looking for.

Once everyone was in place, Mike conferred with Wallace and let her know that the truck in front of the house likely belonged to Jesus Perez.

Wallace nodded and Mike moved into place using a tree for cover, as were the other law enforcement officers. His muscles tensed and his jaw tightened.

After Wallace made sure everyone was ready, another agent used a horn to call out. "This is the DEA. We have you surrounded. Come out slowly, hands up where we can see them." The agent repeated the commands in Spanish.

A moment of silence.

Gunfire erupted from inside the house.

Wood splintered. Glass shattered.

"Shit," Mike said under his breath as he ducked back around the tree.

All bets were off once the occupants of the house started firing at law enforcement officers.

Mike held his Glock in a two-handed grip, peered around the tree, and let off several shots at a shadow that passed a partially boarded up window.

At the same time, agents and deputies also returned fire.

Shouts in Spanish were followed by cries of pain from inside the house and more shots were fired.

An agent near Mike dropped, landing hard on the dark earth. Mike saw the agent clenching his teeth, his back against the tree. The agent reloaded his handgun, ignoring what appeared to be a thigh wound.

More yelling came from inside the house along with more gunfire.

Mike spotted movement to his left as he saw a man dive through a partially boarded window on the south side of the house, not far from Mike.

Perez. Even at the speed the man moved, Mike recognized him.

Betty saw him at the same moment.

Perez bolted between Mike and Betty, into the forest.

"Police!" Mike shouted. "Stop!"

Perez looked over his shoulder, extended his arm, and let off several shots with a handgun.

Betty cried out and Mike saw her go down.

Fury burned hot within Mike and he fired at Perez. The man stumbled and crashed through the underbrush as he moved in and out of the trees. Perez's movements were too erratic for Mike to get off an easy shot.

Perez came back into sight and Mike got off three rounds before Perez dropped.

Gun aimed at Perez, Mike hurried closer.

Perez was facedown, body motionless. Mike couldn't see his weapon.

Mike approached cautiously, his jaw set.

Just as he reached Perez, the man rolled over in a whirl, gun aimed at Mike.

Without hesitation, Mike fired three more rounds into Perez's chest. The man collapsed, his head rolling to the side, eyes wide.

A twig snapped behind Mike. With one eye on Perez, Mike glanced over his shoulder and saw Agent Wallace jogging toward him.

"I've got Perez." Mike crouched, put his fingers to the man's neck and felt for a pulse. Nothing. "He's dead." Wallace came up beside him. "Did you see Turner?"

"One of your other deputies is with her now." Wallace looked grim. "She needs medical attention."

"Damn." Mike started back, jogging to where Ernie was kneeling beside Betty.

Ernie pressed a blood-soaked cloth to Betty's shoulder in a location her body armor couldn't protect her. "Trying to get a few days off?" Ernie said.

Mike knelt on the other side of Betty. "This wouldn't be my first choice of a way to get a doctor's note."

Betty grimaced, her face white. "I'm fine. Just get this big oaf off of me," she said with a nod in Ernie's direction. Even as she gritted her teeth, she added, "Did you get the bastard?"

Mike gave a nod. "He's dead."

Ernie's eyes narrowed. "Good."

A look of satisfaction crossed Betty's features before she bit down on her lower lip.

Sirens approached and Mike raised his head. "I think your ride is here."

"Can we stop for ice cream?" Betty asked with a strained smile. "Make it chocolate. Chocolate makes everything better."

Mike squeezed her uninjured arm. "I'll make sure to get you the good stuff."

Ernie grinned. "We'll even sneak it into the hospital."

"I'm counting on it." Betty gave a weak smile just before her eyes rolled back and her body went slack.

Mike's gut twisted and he felt for her pulse and blew out his breath when he felt the strength of her heartbeat. "Pulse is strong. She passed out."

Ernie nodded. "No doubt from the pain."

"Let's carry her to the clearing," Mike said.

They carefully shifted her so that they could carry her out into the clearing without further damaging her shoulder. They took her to the spot where an ambulance was just pulling up.

Mike and Ernie let the paramedics take over. As much as Mike would like to stay with his deputy and be there for her, he needed to let the professionals take care of her while he did his job.

Thoughts of Kino losing his wife in the fire made Mike think about having a relationship with Anna and how devastating it would be to be in Kino's shoes. It made him all the more determined to get Anna back. He needed her in his life and he knew that she needed him, too.

By the time both crime scenes were dealt with, Mike was beat.

They'd finally taken down Jesus Perez. The bastard would never hurt anyone again.

CHAPTER 23

Anna couldn't take her eyes off of Channel 7 News on her TV screen and tensed as she sat on her living room couch. She watched smoke rising from the smoldering remains of what had housed a meth lab as a news reporter pieced together the details of the explosion.

"We are waiting for the Yavapai County Sheriff's Office to provide us with more information." Paige Windhaven wore a serious expression. "What we've learned so far is that workers in the meth lab are believed to be Mexican nationals, here illegally in the U.S. It is believed that four of the six individuals died in the explosion and two survived. We are working to get more facts to our listeners as soon as possible."

Paige looked directly to the camera. "This is Paige Windhaven, reporting for Channel 7 News."

Brian White, the news anchor, came on screen. "This just in. Another meth lab has been discovered. An unidentified Yavapai County Sheriff's deputy was shot as well as a DEA agent. Suspects were killed in a firefight and arrests have been made. We are waiting for more details on this breaking story."

Anna's heart thumped hard in her chest. Had Mike been involved in the shootings? Could he have been hurt?

She used the remote to click off the news then rubbed her temples with her thumb and forefinger, trying to assuage the ache there.

Mike was in her every other thought. Had he tried calling again? She'd kept her phone off and he hadn't left any messages.

Why would he call her?

Once again she was being irrational and her mind went places it had no business traveling to. She'd screwed up and hurt him not only personally, but professionally as well. She should have known that Chad would let out the truth in exactly the way he had. What a dramatic way to benefit himself by hurting Mike. It had probably been his plan all along.

Her belly clenched and she felt as if she might throw up. She'd felt sick to her stomach every single day since the debate and she wondered if it would ever go away.

For a long sad moment she thought about Chandra, her best friend and Chad's sister. She and Chandra hadn't spoken since Anna had started seeing Mike. So many times she'd wanted to call Chandra and cry on her friend's shoulder.

Not only had she lost her aunt and uncle, but she'd lost Chandra, too. And Mike.

She clenched her jaws. Not Mike. The relationship with him had never been real. She'd been nothing but a pawn in Chad's game and he'd sacrificed her and her family in a deft move.

Her anger with him hadn't dimmed and would eat away at her if she didn't let it go. But how could she? After all that he'd done.

She wasn't sure if it was irrational to still be angry with her aunt and uncle. By coming across illegally, they'd done this to their family. They'd lost their children and they'd torn Anna's heart out. Now she was left to pick up the pieces of her heart as well as Pablo's and Josie's.

Her aunt and uncle had been there for her from the time she came home from college when her parents died, helping her through rough times and the good. She couldn't imagine what her life would have been like without them, but she couldn't help being upset with them because now they weren't going to be here for their children.

It was Sunday afternoon and she and the kids hadn't gone to church that day. They hadn't been back to church since that horrible night. People they knew from the church stopped by to check in on her and her cousins or bring by casseroles and Anna was grateful to know such good people. She never asked anyone in because her emotions were far too raw. She told visitors they were doing well and would be back to church soon.

Anna checked on her young cousins. Pablo was on his bed reading a book with no jacket on it, so she couldn't tell what it was.

"Hi, Pablo." She stepped into his room after knocking on the doorframe. "What are you reading?"

He shrugged. "The City of Ember."

She sat on the edge of his bed, the mattress dipping and squeaking. "Did you get the book from school?"

He nodded, still looking at the book. "Mrs. Marko loaned it to me."

Anna smiled. "You'll have to tell me about it when you're finished."

"Okay," he said, eyes still focused on the book.

Anna squeezed his knee then got up to head to Josie's room.

Josie was sitting on the floor, playing with Barbie dolls, alien action figures, and large-sized Legos in primary colors. Josie loved dolls and spaceships and it looked like she was building a spaceship with the Legos.

Without breaking the silence, Anna sat down with Josie and began building a spaceship, too. Soon Josie started talking, telling Anna about her Barbie dolls going into space and meeting aliens on other planets. The Barbies had tea parties in front of the spaceships and invited the aliens so that they could get to know each other. Anna couldn't help but grin at Josie's vivid imagination.

When the Barbies returned to Earth, Anna stood. Her knees ached after sitting on the floor for so long. "I'm going to make brownies. Sound good to you?"

Josie nodded and smiled. Brownies were one of her favorite treats, something that only Anna had made for the family. "A scoop of vanilla ice cream on top?" Josie asked.

"You bet." Anna smoothed her hand over Josie's hair before leaving the bedroom.

She was almost to the kitchen when the doorbell rang and startled her.

Who could it be? It was probably someone from church with a casserole. The media hadn't bothered her for some time now, so it likely wasn't them. Mike had to be in the middle of the mess that had been reported on TV, and she doubted Chad would show his face around her. As busy as she'd been with her business and family, she hadn't made many friends locally outside of church.

She made her way to the front door, and peered through the peephole. Her eyes widened in surprise.

Chandra.

Her heart thumped against her breastbone as she slid the bolt lock open with a thump. She stepped back as she opened the door.

For a long moment they looked at each other. Chandra's platinum blonde hair was pulled back and she wasn't wearing makeup. She clenched her purse strap like she didn't know what to say.

"Hi, Chandra," Anna finally said.

Chandra's throat worked. "Hi, Anna." Her voice came out sounding broken.

Anna's brow furrowed. "What's wrong?"

"Can I come in?" Chandra hesitated. "Please?"

"Sure." Anna stepped out of the way, feeling off balance, like something was about to go sideways. "Would you like a Coke or water?"

Chandra shook her head. "No thank you."

"You look like you could use something chocolate." Anna offered Chandra a smile. "I have fudge ripple in the freezer."

Chandra managed a smile in return. "First, let's talk."

When they were seated in the living room, Chandra's eyes watered, as if she was about to cry. "I'm so sorry, Anna." A tear rolled down her cheek. "So sorry for everything."

Anna moved to sit beside Chandra and put her arm around her friend, trying to think of what to say.

Chandra lowered her head. "First I overreacted when you started dating Mike McBride. That was none of my business and if our roles had been reversed, I know you wouldn't have acted the way I did."

More tears streaked Chandra's face as she continued, "And worst of all—what Chad did to you and your family." Chandra raised her head, her vivid blue eyes wide and filled with regret. "I never thought he'd say anything about it. I never thought he'd use it against you." Chandra choked back a sob. "I'm so sorry."

Anna brought Chandra into her arms. "You aren't to blame. Don't ever think you are."

"I am." Chandra let out a shuddering sigh as she looked at her hands in her lap. "I let something slip and then ended up telling Chad about your family. He's my twin and he's never broken a confidence with me. Even as children we never told on each other or let anyone else in on our secrets."

"You're not responsible for what Chad does." Anna kept her arm around Chandra's shoulders. "Only he is."

"I know what he did to you." The words came out in a harsh whisper. "I know he blackmailed you."

Anna went still and her gut sickened at the mention of the blackmail, and she couldn't say a word.

Chandra shifted so that she was looking Anna in the eyes again. "I overheard a conversation earlier today between Chad and his campaign manager. Chad talked about how he had forced you to get into a relationship with Mike McBride when he saw that Mike was interested in you. Chad said you'd given him some insider information, too. He and his campaign manager even laughed about the debate and the look on the sheriff's face."

Anger was on Chandra's features now as she continued. "Chad was proud of everything he'd done." She sniffled. "We grew up with Mike and Chad always disliked him. I never dreamed Chad would do anything like this."

Anna had to look away, her own eyes filling with tears. Her words came out choked. "It was—is—such a mess. Everything, a mess."

"I'm so very sorry," Chandra said again. "I know I don't deserve your forgiveness."

Anna wiped tears from her cheek with the back of her hands, trying to compose herself as she turned to face her friend. "Listen to me, Chandra. Chad did something horrible. He twisted it and made it into something ugly and harmful and painful." Anna gripped Chandra's upper arms. "However, *you* did nothing wrong. Do you hear me? *You* did *nothing* wrong."

"But—" Chandra started.

Anna put her hand up, a movement telling her friend to stop. "No more. It is what it is, and it's none of your doing. Okay?"

Chandra said nothing before finally nodding. "Okay. But I should have been here for you with everything you've gone through."

"Stop." Anna hugged Chandra tight and felt her friend's warm tears on her neck. "I'm just glad you're here now."

When Chandra drew back, Anna handed her a tissue box from an end table. Chandra wiped away tears until her face was dry and Anna took a tissue for herself. When both of them had dried their eyes, Anna set the tissue box aside and gave her friend another big hug.

Chandra studied Anna for a long time. "You're in love with him. Mike McBride."

A rush of heat suffused Anna's face. "I don't—I mean he wouldn't…" Anna looked away. "It doesn't matter one way or the other. It's all a big mess."

Chandra put her hand on Anna's arm. "It's true that Mike and I were never close, mostly because Chad hated him." Chandra gave a wry smile. "Mike was always the star and Chad was jealous. Mike excelled at everything he did, and Chad hated him for it." She sighed. "I never dreamed Chad would carry that with him like he has."

"Is that the bad blood between them?" Anna asked before she thought better of it. "Wait, that isn't my business."

Chandra clenched her hands on the tabletop. "One night, when they were in high school, Chad drove a girl named Beth home after a football game. Beth was a good friend to both of them." Chandra stared at her hands. "The next day Beth claimed that Chad had attempted to force himself on her, but she'd managed to get away."

Anna's eyes widened, but said nothing as Chandra continued.

"I've never seen Mike so angry." Chandra shook her head. "He went up to Chad at school, grabbed him by the collar, and hit him. By the time they finished, Chad's nose was broken and he had two black eyes. Mike came away with a bruise on his face, but Chad got the worst of it."

Anna pictured Mike championing the girl. It was something he would do. Chad's nose wasn't crooked, but his family had enough money that likely he had the best surgeon or perhaps he'd had plastic surgery.

Chandra continued, "They were both suspended from school for a couple of weeks for fighting. Beth wouldn't talk about any of it anymore." Chandra let out her breath. "Rumors went around that Beth was paid off by Grandfather or they had hushed her in some other way. I didn't believe it then…but now I don't know."

Despite the fact that she hadn't known Chad when he was younger, Anna wouldn't have been surprised if he and his family had shushed the whole thing. She'd heard stories of some of the Johnsons, that they were cutthroat when they wanted something. As far as Chad was concerned, he'd proven that by blackmailing her.

"Even though there was that bad blood between the two," Chandra went on, "I couldn't help but know Mike was, and always has been, a good guy."

Anna gave a slow nod. "I could tell that from the moment I heard him speak. When we went out for a drink, I had no doubt."

"I wish I could say the same for Chad." Chandra looked pained. "I love my brother, but he can be ruthless when it comes to getting what he wants. I just never could have believed he'd stoop to this level." She met Anna's gaze. "I don't know what to do about it. I feel like I need to make this right."

"You shouldn't do anything." Anna squeezed her friend's hand. "I believe in karma. What Chad does and has done will come back to him in some way."

"You're probably right." Chandra let out a sigh. "My own brother. I don't know if I can look him in the face again. What do I do?"

"I won't come between you two," Anna said. "You need to make your own decisions when it comes to Chad. Does the good between you two outweigh the bad things he's done?"

"I don't know. Maybe this means that I can't trust a man who would do something so horrible like this to anyone." Chandra shook her head, her blonde ponytail bobbing side to side. "He's not the man I knew. Or loved." She clenched her fists on her lap. "I'm so—so *angry* with him."

"Give yourself some time to think this through." Anna took Chandra's hands in hers. "Don't make any decisions while you're angry and upset."

Chandra nodded. "You're right. But I am going to confront him. I just don't know how or when."

Anna squeezed Chandra's hands in hers.

Chandra let out her breath. "Now, about you and Mike."

Anna went still. "What about him?"

"Have you talked with him since everything went to hell?" Chandra asked.

With a shake of her head, Anna said, "No."

Chandra tilted her head to the side. "Has he tried calling you?"

"Yes." Anna swallowed. "But I ignored his calls and I turned my phone off."

"You need to talk to him and let him know how you feel." Chandra looked earnestly into Anna's eyes. "I'll bet he feels the same way."

Heat flushed Anna's cheeks. "After everything that happened, I doubt it."

"We'll figure this out." Chandra gave a decisive nod. "In the meantime, tell me how you and the kids are doing."

"How about some fudge ripple?" Anna released Chandra's hands and stood. "Brand new carton."

"You bet." Chandra stood, too. She linked her arm through Anna's, just like the days before everything went to hell, and they headed into the kitchen.

CHAPTER 24

Monday morning Mike frowned as he sat in his desk in his office and read through the news on his iPad—the *Prescott Valley Tribune* and the *Arizona Republic*. Both had articles on him and the weekend's activities.

He was being regaled as a hero because he'd saved his sister-in-law's life at the Halloween party and because the YCSO, along with the DEA, had brought down three meth houses in addition to the one that had gone up in flames. Suspected—and notorious to Prescott residents—drug smuggler and human trafficker, Jesus Perez, was dead and it had been reported that Mike had been the one to shoot him.

"Hero. Shit." Mike rubbed his temples. He didn't like one damned bit that the news had recorded him performing the Heimlich maneuver on Ricki. It was no one's business, certainly not all of Yavapai County. And the whole damned sheriff's department and DEA had worked together to find Perez's meth houses. He'd made a public statement acknowledging those facts.

Mike set the tablet down and pushed his fingers through his hair. He'd had his reservations about bringing the press to the family Halloween party and regretted it now. He hoped that Ricki wasn't too embarrassed. Garrett had been nothing but grateful and told Mike he owed him big time. Mike said nothing was owed to him and that everyone in the family would have done it in a heartbeat, which was the truth.

This morning, before her bakery opened, Ricki had brought over a box of Mike's favorite, freshly made, pastries. She'd hugged him and thanked him with tears sparkling in her eyes and he'd hugged her back before she'd turned and left his office.

He couldn't imagine Ricki not being part of the family and was damned glad he'd been in the right place at the right time. Not only losing her, but losing the baby too would have devastated the family.

Ricki and her pregnancy made him think of Anna again. He wanted to talk to her so damned badly. But it hadn't even been two weeks yet. Hard to believe so little time had passed with as much as had happened.

"Mike?" A voice from the direction of his doorway caught his attention and he looked up. He was surprised to see Chandra Johnson, his opponent's twin sister. "I mean, Sheriff," she said. She appeared hesitant. "May I come in and talk with you a moment?"

Mike stood and gestured to a seat in front of his desk. "Come on in."

When Chandra was seated in front of his desk, Mike sat and rested his hands on the desktop. "Long time no see. How've you been?"

She looked surprised, as if she hadn't expected him to be friendly. "I'm doing well." She tucked behind her ear a strand of blonde hair the color of corn silk before clutching her purse in her lap. "I saw that you've had a busy weekend."

"You could say that." Mike gave a nod. "What can I do for you?"

Chandra's throat worked. "It's about Chad and Anna."

Mike held back a frown. The fact that Chandra had put the two names together in the same sentence put him on guard.

She bit her lower lip before taking a deep breath and saying in a rush, "Chad blackmailed Anna."

A bolt of shock went through Mike followed by a surge of anger toward Chad that was so great he felt a vein pulse in his forehead. "What do you mean, Chad blackmailed Anna?"

Chandra shifted uneasily in her seat, her features strained. "Yesterday I overheard him talking to his campaign manager. Earlier this month, he told Anna that if she didn't get close to you, he would tell the authorities about her aunt and uncle being here illegally."

Mike's skin went cold as he tried to process the information. Anna had gotten close to him because Chad had blackmailed her. Thoughts burned through his mind. *Anna, blackmailed. Forced to get close to him. Was it all an act? Every damned bit of it?*

But then his thoughts switched to what Chad had done.

"I think at first Anna started meeting with you and working for your campaign office because that's what Chad ordered her to do." Chandra rubbed her hands on her slacks. "But I truly believe that Anna fell in love with you along the way."

For a moment Mike felt completely lost. "How did you arrive at that?"

"Anna and I have been close friends since she moved to Prescott." Chandra clenched her purse in her lap. "When I found out that she had gone out with you for drinks, I got angry because you're my brother's opponent. I hadn't spoken with her for weeks— not until yesterday, when I went to see her after overhearing my brother talk about the blackmail."

Mike said nothing as he tried to piece together his memories of his times with Anna over the past few weeks along with this new information.

"Anna was scared because of Chad's threats, scared because you're the sheriff and her family was here illegally." Chandra leaned forward in her seat. "And scared because after all of that, she had fallen in love with you and she knew there was no future in it. She didn't want to hurt you and she didn't want to lose her family."

"She must have been going through hell." Mike couldn't imagine that much turmoil going through one person. He clenched his hands into fists. "If Chad was here right now, I'd—"

"Do nothing," Chandra cut in. "Don't think that I don't believe he deserves a good ass-kicking. But you'd lose your job and probably end up in jail. My brother may be a lot of things, but he's also a damned good lawyer."

Despite the fact Mike knew she was right, it didn't make it any easier. He took in a deep breath and let it out. "How is Anna? I haven't been able to reach her and I don't want to stop by her house without her knowing I'm coming by. More for the kids' sake. They're going through a hell of a lot without a man in law enforcement stopping by."

"Anna is doing as well as can be expected." Chandra sighed. "Her busy season for her event business is starting up for the holidays and she's trying to work on each event while spending time with the kids. She's gone from a household of adults with two children, to being the sole support system for the kids."

Mike nodded. He'd been thinking the same. "What do I need to do to get her to talk to me?"

"Wait until Thanksgiving." Chandra looked at him earnestly. "That's not too far, and waiting will allow you to spend time where you need to put it right now—the election is only a week away. It will also give her a little more time to get used to the changes in her life."

"How do I get her to talk to me?" Mike asked. "If it wasn't for the kids, I'd be knocking on her door right this minute. Hell, I would have done it already. But I don't want to take the chance of upsetting the kids."

"I've already invited myself over for Thanksgiving," Chandra said. "I'll tell her I'm bringing a friend. We'll go early so you can talk with Anna before dinner."

Mike thought about it a moment. With the way things were, it might be the only way to take Anna aside and talk with her. It would give her and the kids a little more time to adjust to her new situation.

He gave a slow nod. "All right."

"Good." Chandra beamed and got to her feet as she swung her purse over her shoulder. She hesitated, her smile fading a little. "I'm so sorry about what Chad did to both of you."

"You aren't your brother's keeper." Mike walked around his desk and stood in front of Chandra. He took her by the shoulders. "Thank you for coming."

"You're welcome." She gave Mike a quick hug. "I'll call you after the election to set everything up."

He reached into his shirt pocket and brought out a business card. He took a pen from his desk and wrote a number on the back before handing the card to her. "That's my personal mobile phone."

She tucked the card in her purse. "I'll be talking with you soon."

After Chandra left, Mike returned to his desk and sat in his chair, leaning back into it. Heated fury still burned beneath Mike's skin. He wanted to beat the shit out of Chad Johnson for all that he'd done to Anna, but Chandra was right. The last thing he needed was to be thrown in jail.

He didn't know if it was wrong to surprise Anna like he and Chandra had planned it, but it was all he had right now and he'd take it.

CHAPTER 25

Her home smelled of the holidays. Anna took in a deep breath of all the aromas. Smells of hot homemade bread, a stuffed turkey baking in the oven and sweet potatoes in brown sugar filled the air. She'd also placed bowls of holiday potpourri around the house that made everything feel more like fall.

It was a gorgeous day outside, the air still and cool and the sky blue with just a few wispy clouds scattered across the sky. The weather was supposed to turn over the weekend, with rain and possibly snow in the forecast. However, today it was beautiful.

Chandra had asked to spend Thanksgiving with them, probably because she didn't want Anna and the kids to be alone, and maybe partly because she was so mad at her brother.

Mike had won the election in a landslide victory and Anna would bet that Chad wouldn't be pleasant to be around.

To top it off, during last night's newscast, the reporter had stated Chad was under investigation for improprieties during the election. Bribes and blackmail were words that had been tossed around, but nothing concrete had been said. Yet.

Did the blackmail allegations have anything to do with what Chad did to Anna? Or had he been up to more than she was aware of or capable of imagining?

Karma, she thought. Chad's true colors had shown through all the wealth and power that he and the Johnson family had.

Thoughts of Mike sent pangs through her belly. She hadn't seen him since that awful night and he'd stopped calling. She knew it was for the best, but the sense of loss was so great that it was as bad as losing her aunt and uncle all over again. She might have only known Mike for a short time, but her heart and soul had known him forever.

Pablo and Josie walked back into the kitchen from the dining room. They had visited with their mamá and papá via Skype earlier in the day. They spoke with their parents nearly every evening before bedtime.

"The table is set for five people," Josie said. "Who is Chandra bringing with her?"

"I don't know." Anna put the fresh bread into the breadbasket and covered it with a cloth. "She asked me at the last minute and didn't stay on the phone long enough to tell me."

"What else do you want us to do?" Pablo asked. He had been so reserved since his parents were deported. Sometimes he acted up but he seemed to be settling into the routine a little better now.

"Why don't you go play a board game?" Anna smiled. "It will be another hour and a half before we eat and you've done a great job of helping with cleaning and setting the table."

"Josie only wants to play little kid board games," Pablo said.

Josie put her hands on her hips. "Do not."

Anna held her hands up. "You both like Monopoly, so compromise and play the junior version of the game."

"Yay!" Josie bounced on the balls of her feet and clapped her hands. "I'll go get it."

Pablo rolled his eyes but Anna saw the hint of a smile. "All right," he said before following his sister out of the kitchen. Just as he crossed the threshold into the living room, the doorbell rang. "I'll get it," he called out.

Anna went to the fridge and opened the door. She leaned in and grabbed a head of romaine lettuce, baby carrots, tomatoes, an avocado, and a bag of orange, red, and yellow sweet peppers. With her arms full, she rose up, bumped her hip into the door to close it, then turned—and dropped everything.

Mike was standing two steps away.

Tomatoes and avocados rolled. The romaine fell to her feet. The bags of peppers and carrots opened, scattering the contents across the floor.

Heat rushed to her cheeks and her entire body tingled as she stared at him, her lips parted in surprise.

His brown eyes were dark with an emotion she couldn't read. She drank in the cut of his features, the power in his build, the strength of his presence.

Without giving her a chance to think or react beyond that one moment, he brought her into his arms, captured her mouth with his, and kissed her.

So much longing and need for him was built up inside her. She wrapped her arms around his neck and kissed him in return.

It was a deep, hard, and long kiss. There was almost a desperation to it, as if they could never get enough, and as if they might be torn apart again if they didn't hold on tight.

He held her close, his hard body warming hers. He felt so solid and real yet she almost felt like she was dreaming. He was here and she was in his arms.

When he drew away, her heart was pounding hard, her breaths coming short and shallow. She stared into his eyes, still unable to believe that he really was there and she was in his arms.

He kissed her again, as if he couldn't get enough of her. As if he was afraid she might disappear, leaving his arms empty.

"Anna." He crushed her to him. "God, how I've missed you."

"I've missed you, too." She placed her hands on his chest and looked up at him. "After what happened, I didn't think I'd ever be able to face you again. But here you are."

He rested his hands on her hips. "I would have been here long before, but I was sure you needed time to get adjusted."

"I did. We did." She kept her palms pressed against the hard wall of muscle of his chest. "Everything has changed."

He brushed his knuckles across her cheek. "You won't go through anything else alone. I'm here now and I'm not going anywhere."

Tears pushed at the backs of her eyes and one leaked down her cheek. "Thank you."

He wiped away the tear with his thumb. "I'm sorry you went through all that you did. I wish there was some way I could make it better."

"You're here." She slid her hands up to his shoulders. "That is everything to me." She glanced away, unable to look into his eyes for a long moment. When she turned her gaze back to his, she said, "There's something I have to tell you." Her voice wavered. "I don't know if you'll still care for me once I tell you."

"Shhh." He put his fingers to her lips. "Chandra told me what Chad put you through to get to me. I'm so sorry about all that he did and how badly it hurt you."

"It was a nightmare." She swallowed. "And since then it's been like a waking dream I haven't been able to come out of. Are you part of that dream?"

"I'm real." He cupped her face. "You're real." He moved his mouth softly over hers before raising his head. "And I love you, Anna. I love you with everything I have."

Her eyes widened and she felt like her entire body was aflame. "I love you, Mike." She threw her arms around his neck and held on tight. "I love you so much. It killed me to know that I could hurt you. And then it happened, in the worst way possible."

He drew back and held her gaze. "Nothing good came out of that night and I know you've been through hell since then. From here on out we'll make it as right as we can and we'll do it together. You won't face the future alone again."

More tears threatened to fall. "I love you so much."

"Not any more than I love you." He smiled and looked around their feet. "I never imagined this moment being in the middle of salad makings."

Anna gave a half-sob, half-laugh as she wiped an errant tear from her eye and smiled. "I never allowed myself to imagine a moment like this with you. This will always be one of my most precious memories."

"We'll make lots more." He dug into his pocket and pulled out a brown velvet ring box.

Her breath caught in her throat as she looked from the ring box to him. His expression serious, he knelt on one knee amongst the produce and opened the box. A beautiful solitaire diamond ring was nestled in the chocolate brown velvet.

His gaze held hers. "Anna, will you marry me?"

Her legs gave out and she went down on both knees in front of him. Thoughts whirled through her mind. She wanted to scream, "Yes!" But instead she said, "I have the kids now. I'm adopting them. I can't expect you to become an instant parent."

"I want to be a parent with you." Mike searched her gaze. "I want to raise Josie and Pablo as our own. And I want to give them younger siblings to grow up with."

Anna wasn't sure she could breathe, much less speak.

"Say yes, Anna." He hooked his finger under her chin. "I want to be with you for the rest of our days."

In a voice choked with emotion, she said, "Yes." Then louder and more clearly, "Yes, I will marry you."

He slid the ring on her finger. For a long moment she stared at it, the ring sparkling in the kitchen lighting like prisms of fire.

They kissed again before the sound of applause jerked them apart. They looked to see Josie, Pablo, and Chandra standing in the doorway, all three of them grinning.

Anna held her arms wide and both her young cousins ran toward them and Anna wrapped them in her embrace.

After a long hug, Mike brought Anna to her feet and rested his arm around her waist, drawing her close, and she leaned into his strength and warmth.

They kissed again and flashes brought them out of the kiss. Pablo was taking pictures with Anna's cell phone, and Chandra appeared to be recording them.

"This goes on Facebook," Chandra said with a grin.

"Noooo," Anna said in a sudden panic.

"Just kidding." Chandra's grin broadened. "But you will have it for posterity."

"Come here." Anna gestured to the kids and crouched on the floor, Mike along with them.

Anna took her cell phone from Pablo and handed it to Mike, who seemed to know exactly what she wanted him to do. He stretched out his arm and took their first family selfie.

When he showed it to them and Anna saw their four smiling faces, she grinned. "Best. Selfie. Ever."

Chandra laughed. "And may there be many more."

Anna and Mike looked at each other. He said, "We're just getting started."

ALSO BY CHEYENNE MCCRAY

Paranormal

Dark Seduction
Night's Captive
Future Knight

Lexi Steele Novels

The First Sin
The Second Betrayal
The Temptation

~Romantic Erotica~

"Seraphine Chronicles" Series

Forbidden
Bewitched
Spellbound
(*Spellbound* includes bonus novella, *Untamed*)
Possessed

From St. Martin's Press:

"Night Tracker" Series

Demons Not Included
No Werewolves Allowed
Vampires Not Invited
Zombies Sold Separately
Vampires Dead Ahead
No Cursed Allowed—novella (in the Demons & Lovers
collection)

Cheyenne writing as Jaymie Holland

"Tattoos and Leather" ménage

Inked

Branded

"Hearts in Chains" BDSM Series

Wounded

"The Auction" Series

Sold

Bought

Claimed (with bonus novella *Taken*)

"Taboo" Series

Wicked Nights: three Erotic Tales

Taboo Desires: three Tales of Lust and Passion

Playing Rough: three Stories of Sensual Submission

Paranormal

The Touch

Excerpt... Held By You

Cheyenne McCray

"See you, Ricki," Hollie Simmons called out to the owner of Sweet Things Bakery. Hollie juggled two large pink boxes of holiday cookies as she pressed her hip against the glass door of the bakery. "Merry Christmas."

Ricki gave a little wave. "Bye, Hollie. Hope those kiddos of yours enjoy the goodies."

Before Hollie could push the door open with her hip, it swung wide, catching Hollie off guard. She stumbled out of the bakery and gave a little cry, knowing in that instant that she and her cookies were going to land hard and scatter across the sidewalk.

A man's strong arm caught her around her shoulders, dragging her up against a hard chest. At the same time her savior caught her, he caught the cookies in his opposite hand, gracefully saving them from their fate of moments before.

"Oh! Thank you." Hollie let out a breath of relief as the unseen man steadied her. The bakery door closed, leaving her on the sidewalk with the man who still held her. She caught a sexy masculine scent that was warm despite the December chill in the air. She tried to turn but he didn't immediately set her free, ensuring she was steady on her feet.

He dropped his arm from around her shoulders but kept his hold on the cookies. She turned and hitched her purse up on her shoulder. It was Lieutenant John McBride who had just saved her from a nasty fall.

"Lieutenant McBride." For no reason whatsoever, her stomach gave a little flip. Okay, maybe there was a reason…and that reason was wrapped up in a six-foot-two, brown-eyed, dark-haired package wearing a uniform fitted to perfection on a powerfully muscled body. "Thanks so much."

"It was my fault." He shook his head. "I didn't see you and I opened the door at the same time you were coming out."

"Whatever the case, thanks for catching me." She smiled. "Protect and serve. You're doing a great job of it."

He gave a little grin that surprised her. She didn't know the police lieutenant personally, but whenever she had seen him, he had never been wearing a smile. He always seemed so serious. That hadn't stopped her from having a little crush on him from afar. She'd always found the man incredibly attractive from a distance. His seriousness, his hard expression, had made her want to know more about the man and what made him tick.

She'd always been too shy to go up to him and introduce herself when she'd seen him around town. With her full curves, and stepbrothers who had belittled her constantly since she was a child, her confidence wasn't the best.

Lieutenant McBride raised the boxes of cookies. "Let me take these to your car."

"Thanks." She nodded toward her small Honda parked along the curb.

He walked at her side as she headed for the car. "Are these for your students?" His question surprised her and she cut her gaze to his. "I imagine today you're having holiday parties at the elementary school."

She blinked. "You know who I am?"

He gave a slow grin. "How could I not know one of the best kindergarten teachers in the school district, Ms. Simmons? You have an excellent reputation."

"I could say the same about you." She couldn't help but smile again as they reached the car's driver's side door, which she unlocked with the remote. "But it is nice to actually meet you in person."

He gave a nod and opened the car door for her with one hand, still holding the cookie boxes with his other. Before she could extend her hands to take the boxes from him, he leaned past her, into her car, and set the cookies on the passenger seat.

When he drew back, his body brushed hers. She felt a shiver run through her that had absolutely nothing to do with the cold, and she swallowed as her body reacted to his nearness. She wanted her few moments with John McBride to last. She wasn't ready to part company with him yet...and she wanted to see him again. Now how could she possibly arrange that?

A thought came to her and she cleared her throat. "After the holidays, I'm having a career day in my class. Do you think you might have time in your schedule to visit my children?"

John studied her in a way that made her stomach flip. She found herself holding her breath as if she'd just asked him out on a date.

He gave a slow nod. "I'd enjoy that."

She let out her breath in a rush. "So would I—I mean the children."

Again a sexy little smile. "Why don't I call you and we'll set up a date and time?"

"Sure." She tried to compose herself after her slip up and clasped the strap of her purse for something to do with her hands as he pulled a small spiral-bound notebook from his shirt pocket. "Going to put me in there with all of your suspects and criminals?"

This time he gave a low laugh. "I have a section reserved just for you."

A flutter went through her midsection again. Was he flirting with her? Yes, he was definitely flirting with her.

She gave him her number and he jotted it down before tucking the notepad into his uniform pocket again. He pulled out a business card with a police shield, Prescott Police Department, and his name and number on it. She held onto the card as she looked up at him.

"You have a good day, Ms. Simmons," he said.

"Please call me Hollie," she said. "I hope your day is great too."

He gave a nod. "Hollie." The way he said her name about made her melt. His voice was warm and deep and at that moment had a caress to it. She had no doubt that his tone would turn hard in a flash when necessary.

It didn't surprise her that he didn't tell her to call him by his first name. After all, she didn't know him well and he was an officer of the law and had to maintain a certain amount of distance in public.

She gave him one last smile before climbing into her car. She dropped his business card into her purse as he closed the door behind her.

After she turned on her car, he watched her back out of her parking space. His presence made her so nervous she almost backed into a passing car and she had to jam her foot on the brake pedal. Her face flushed with heat and she did her best not to look at John McBride as she guided her vehicle out of the spot and headed toward the elementary school.

Excerpt... Made For You

Cheyenne McCray

Reese broke the kiss and Kelley found herself breathing hard as his gaze held hers. He cupped her face with one hand and brushed his thumb over her cheek. "You are something else, Kelley."

"What?" she asked, her voice low and breathy.

"You're so special to me." He lowered his head and their lips met again.

She could almost swear fireworks sparked behind her closed eyelids as he kissed her. It was a kiss like nothing she'd ever experienced before, a kiss she never wanted to end.

He scooped her into his arms, catching her off guard. She clung to his neck and he swept her out of the kitchen and down a hall, his stride long and deliberate. When he reached what she guessed was the master bedroom, he pushed the door open and set her on her feet on a hunter green rug next to a rustic four-poster bed. He swept aside the pillow from the top of the plaid comforter and pulled the comforter back with one hand.

Her insides tingled and then he was kissing her again while exploring her body with his fingertips. His touch was gentle when it came to her shoulder, but he pulled her tight up against him so that she felt the hard ridge of his erection against her belly.

He picked her up by her waist and set her on the edge of the mattress. She watched him, hunger growing within her as he knelt in front of her and tugged off one of her leather shoes and then the other. His gaze met hers as he peeled off each of her socks.

When her feet were bare, he caressed then before sliding his hands up her calves, over her jeans, on up to her thighs. The heat of his palms burned through the denim to her flesh. His hands continued on to the button of her jeans.

She couldn't take her eyes off him, her heart pounding faster with every movement he made. She braced her hands on the mattress and leaned back. Butterflies skittered through her belly as she raised her hips so that he could pull her jeans down.

Her breath caught in her throat as he removed her jeans, leaving her in her black panties. Still on his knees, he pressed his big body between her thighs, pushing them apart.

"Your skin is so soft." He skimmed his palms along her legs, causing goose bumps to rise up on her flesh. "I didn't know how much I wanted to touch you until this moment." His blue eyes held hers. "And now I don't think I can get enough."

She shivered as he said the words and he moved his hands over her hips, sliding over the silk of her panties to the hem of her white T-shirt.

"Is your shoulder going to be okay if we take this off?" he said as he paused.

She raised her arms. "My shoulder is fine now."

Still, he carefully eased the T-shirt over her head and arms. When the shirt was off, he set it aside, and he looked at her, taking in her black panties and matching satin and lace bra.

She bit her lower lip as he traced the line of her bra, skimming her breasts with his callused fingers. Her entire body grew sensitized, his every touch making her want him that much more.

He watched her as he cupped her breasts and ran his thumbs over her satin-covered nipples. They tightened and ached and she wanted nothing more than to feel the warmth of his mouth on them.

Unable to move her gaze from his, she arched her back, pressing her breasts against his palms. His eyes seemed to burn like blue flame as he reached behind her and unfastened her bra. He slid the straps down her arms and bared her breasts.

Excerpt... Inked

"Tattoos and Leather" bondage ménage series
by Jaymie Holland

They were here again.

Double Trouble. Two-riffic. Twice Blessed.

Megan Faircloth had a lot of nicknames for the twins, never mind the wicked fantasies they triggered every time they strolled past the room of typists at Dorian International Imports.

She sat in her tiny cubby to the left of the door and forced herself to keep her head turned toward her computer screen. It was no good, though. Her eyes kept darting to the dark-haired gods as they sat on the visitor's couch near the entrance to the executive suites. She carefully dislodged one of her ear buds so she could hear the men if they said anything.

They never did.

Tall, dark, and handsome—check. Hard, muscular bodies beneath those suits—she'd bet her grandmother's photograph on it.

And silent as two chiseled stones, they never said a word.

They had to be identical, not just fraternal. They were the same height. They wore the same expensive-looking charcoal suits, and both of them carried dark brown leather briefcases. Their black hair was the same length, cut close, but not too close. They even had the same eyes, blue as sapphires, hard and wary as they scanned the halls before taking iPads out of their briefcases and getting to work.

Megan imagined their Facebook pages. Handsome and Just as Handsome. No, wait. Sexiest Twins on Earth.

They probably had names like Dirk and Rock.

And their Facebook pages would be private anyway. No droolers allowed.

She had no idea why the men had been coming to DII every Friday for the last two months, but she wasn't complaining. It was the only excitement she'd had in weeks.

Dead-end job. Dead-end life. She sighed and tried again to focus on the letter she was supposed to be typing.

Men like those two would never give her a second look. They were the types to drink champagne with supermodels on private planes jetting to Madagascar, not hang out with administrative assistants who had nothing to offer but curves, freckles, and a big smile.

Megan put her fingers back on the keyboard and corrected a couple of obvious typos. It wasn't like she planned to spend her life doing office work, but she didn't have the money to finish college and there was no rich relative to foot the bill. Hell, she barely had the money to make rent. Her roommate, Drew Holloway, kept trying to get her to sign up as a consultant to throw Sweet Sensations parties, but just thinking about doing something like that—heat rose to Megan's cheeks.

Her eyes drifted from her computer monitor, back to the gorgeous suits and muscles outside her door, and—

Oh, God.

One of them was staring at her.

Her entire body went rigid as Twin One's blue eyes fixed on hers and held her gaze. Megan's breathing nearly stopped, and her pulse pounded fast in her throat. Her cheeks had been warm before, but they flamed now, and she felt the hot blush kiss her neck, even her ears. She had never had such a total full-on view of one of the twins, and she noticed something on the left side of this one's neck. A dark swirl, or some sort of mark. Maybe a thorn?

Was that a tattoo?

Megan's thoughts instantly rushed to what he would look like with that jacket off and his pressed shirt unbuttoned to show her the full cut of his abs—and the pattern of his ink.

What would a man like that tattoo on his chest?

I'm losing it.

Twin Two slowly raised his eyes from his iPad. Megan's gaze shifted wildly between the men as they both examined her from foot to knee to hip, and higher. She wished she had worn something sexier than her comfortable khaki skirt and her old short-sleeved pink sweater, but their expressions left little doubt that her clothes hid nothing from them.

And her screaming blush didn't do much to deny her interest, did it?

Then she realized they had focused on her dislodged ear bud, as if they both knew she had been hoping to eavesdrop on their conversation.

Twin One lifted one finger and made a tsk-tsk movement.

Twin Two's lips twitched into the barest hint of a smile.

Megan thought she might die right where she sat, of embarrassment, of pathetic desire, she didn't even know which would be fatal faster.

The executive suite door opened, shattering the moment.

Megan jumped. She crammed her ear bud back in place and positioned her fingers on the keyboard, tapping mindlessly and hoping she didn't look too guilty.

A man in a blue suit greeted the twins with handshakes. They stood and tucked their iPads back into their leather briefcases. Without giving her a second glance, they strolled after the man in the blue suit, letting the door swing shut behind them.

Gone.

Just like that.

Why did that make her want to scream?

Something is seriously wrong with me, she thought. Then, unable to help herself, she typed, *Gorgeous.* Then, *Delicious!*

She deleted the words and put her face in her hands.

Breathe. That's it. Nice and slow...

It took a while to get back on track, but Megan finally managed. She had trouble not glancing at the doors to the executive suite, though. Five minutes went by between checks, then ten. Half an hour. An hour.

Sooner or later, the twins would come back through, and when they did, maybe they would notice her again...

ABOUT CHEYENNE

New York Times and *USA Today* bestselling author Cheyenne McCray's books have received multiple awards and nominations, including

RT Book Reviews magazine's Reviewer's Choice awards for Best Erotic Romance of the year and Best Paranormal Action Adventure of the year

*Three "RT Book Reviews" nominations, including Best Erotic Romance, Best Romantic Suspense, and Best Paranormal Action Adventure.

*Golden Quill award for Best Erotic Romance

*The Road to Romance's Reviewer's Choice Award

*Gold Star Award from Just Erotic Romance Reviews

*CAPA award from The Romance Studio

Cheyenne grew up on a ranch in southeastern Arizona. She has been writing ever since she can remember, back to her kindergarten days when she penned her first poem. She always knew one day she would write novels, hoping her readers would get lost in the worlds she created, just as she experienced when she read some of her favorite books.

Chey has three sons, two dogs, and is an Arizona native who loves the desert, the sunshine, and the beautiful sunsets. Visit Chey's website and get all of the latest info at her website and meet up with her at Cheyenne McCray's Place on Facebook!